Nidor.
Nidor, one of two continents on a water-covered planet
Nidor, a planet, a people, a nation
Nidor, a religion . . .

THE DAWNING LIGHT

Also by Robert Randall

THE SHROUDED PLANET

ROBERT SILVERBERG & RANDALL GARRETT
WRITING AS
ROBERT RANDALL

THE DAWNING LIGHT

SF
ACE BOOKS, NEW YORK

An Ace Book

Published by arrangement with Starblaze Editions/The Donning Company

ISBN: 0-441-13898-5

First Ace Printing: October 1982
Published simultaneously in Canada

Manufactured in the United States of America

Ace Books, 200 Madison Avenue, New York, New York 10016

*To that team without whom this book
would never have been written:*

G & S

THE DAWNING LIGHT

PROLOGUE

After seven centuries of search, *homo sapiens* of Earth
finally found the planet, the race, that was needed. The
dominant race of Earth had passed the time of its
adolescence and was approaching maturity. But maturity implies wisdom, and, in this instance, wisdom dictated the need of a partner—another race, neither too
much like Man nor too different from him. The planet
Nidor provided just such a race.

Nidor's primary was a B class star, a huge, blue-white
stellar engine that poured out radiation at a rate that
made Earth's Sol look picayune in comparison. Nidor
swung round that ferociously glaring furnace at a distance so great that it took nearly three thousand years
for the world to complete one revolution—and, even
so, the planet was hot. The continents, just south of the
equator, had a mean temperature of 110° Fahrenheit,
and a climate that varied but little from the mean.

There was comparatively little dry land: more than
eighty-five percent of the planet's surface was covered
by the shallow sea whose tides moved gently beneath
the eternally cloudfilled sky, pulled by the gravitational
field of the single nearby moon.

Geological evidence indicated that the planet had, some four thousand years before, gone through a period of upheaval during which whole continents had sunk beneath the waters. It was upon the legend of the events at that time that the religion and the culture of Nidor was built.

Before the Cataclysm, the planet had evolved humanoids physically very similar to Man; to the eye, the only major difference was that instead of the irregular distribution of hair over his body that is so characteristic of the Earthman, the Nidorian's light, curly down was fairly evenly distributed over his body, and ranged in color from platinum blonde to light brown.

After the Cataclysm, the sole remaining group of civilized beings on the planet were on the small continent of Nidor; to the Nidorians, that continent and its offshore islands constituted the entire world. All the rest was occupied by the Demons of Darkness beyond the sea.

The history of the Nidorians stretched back no further than the Great Cataclysm, a period in history dominated by the legendary figure of the Great Lawyer, Belrogas Yorgen, who had brought the Sixteen Clans to safety during the planetary upheaval that had destroyed so much life on land and in the sea. It was the great Bel-rogas—so legend said—who had given Nidor its government, its religion, and its Sacred Scriptures.

Politically, Nidor was a theocracy, ruled by the Elder Grandfathers, a council of the sixteen elder priests, the eldest priest of each of the Sixteen Clans being automatically a member of the Council, and the eldest of these automatically becoming the Elder Leader of the Council. The decisions of the Council of Elders were final and binding, but they were far from arbitrary. Each decision was based upon precedent and the Sacred Scriptures. It was a balanced, static society, operating on age-old laws and taboos.

The religion itself was an ethical code centering on a worship of the Great Light, the cloud-shrouded sun of Nidor, and controlled by the Grandfathers—the priests of Nidor.

The Nidorian "year" was not, of course, based on the revolution of the planet about its primary, but on multiples of the rotation of the planet about its axis, which required twenty-four hours and some odd minutes by Terrestrial computation. Sixteen of these days made a period, sixteen periods made a year, and sixteen years made a cycle. According to the Nidorian calendar, therefore, the Earthmen made themselves known on the first day of the first year—the Year of Yorgen—of the 240th Cycle since the Great Cataclysm.

Down they came in their great silvery ship, seemingly descending from the Great Light Himself, to a spot some miles from the capital of Nidor, the Holy City of Gelusar. Representing themselves as agents of the Great Light, they had announced that a school was to be built on that spot—the Bel-rogas School of Divine Law. Only the best of Nidor's younger students would be allowed to come to the co-educational school, young men and women with high scholastic attainments and good health. And the Council of Elders agreed.

Two Cycles after its establishment, the school produced the first of its great men, Kiv peGanz Brajjyd—Kiv, the son of Ganz, of the Clan Brajjyd. While still in school, Kiv had brought fame to himself by finding a way to eradicate the *hugl,* a crop-eating pest which had mutated suddenly to become even more dangerous than before. Edris powder, which had controlled the pest for thousands of years, no longer seemed to be lethal to the adult *hugl,* but Kiv, having studied the life cycle of the little creatures, was able to show that they could be wiped out by using Edris powder on them while they were still in the pre-adult stage.

The fact that this partially upset the ecology and economy of Nidor weighed heavily on Kiv's mind, but as the situation adjusted itself to a new balance, he managed to dismiss it from his thoughts. Eventually, he entered the Sacred Priesthood, and before another two Cycles had passed, his daughter, Sindi, had enrolled in the Bel-rogas School.

Sindi, like her father, was an innovator; unlike him, her innovation was in the sociological, rather than the scientific field. She fell in love with another Brajjyd, in violation of the injunction against in-clan marriages. As a result of her marriage and that between two members of the great Yorgen Clan, the injunction was discarded.

The third innovator of the family was Norvis peRahn Brajjyd, son of Sindi and grandson of Kiv. Norvis, exploring the field of biochemistry under the tutelage of the long-lived Earthmen, discovered a hormone which, when applied to the peych-bean—the staple crop of Nidor—would almost double its rate of growth. Here, he thought, was the discovery that would bring him the fame and success that his mother's father, Elder Grandfather Kiv, had achieved.

His hopes were wrecked by the Earthman, Smith, who had been working with him on the hormone project. Smith stole the notes on the work and gave full credit for the invention to another student at the school, while Norvis was summarily dismissed for saying that the Earthman, who was accepted as an Emissary of the Great Light, was a thief and a liar.

After narrowly escaping death from stoning for blasphemy, Norvis fled from Holy Gelusar, changing his name to Norvis peKrin Dmorno, to leave the impression that Norvis peRahn was actually dead.

The hormone was made in small quantities and sold to the Elders, but the Elders' farms produced more peych than normal, thus driving down the price and putting the smaller farmers out of business.

Feeling that it was unjust to keep the hormone from the smaller farmers, Norvis, with the aid of a free-thinking old sea captain named Del peFenn Vyless, secretly made the hormone and distributed it to farmers all over Nidor.

The unforeseen result was an economic collapse that took fourteen years to straighten out. Deluged by a surfeit of food and peych-fiber, which became worth-less in their plenty, and plagued by the excess of animal life which resulted, Nidor fell into the Great Depress-ion. Another unsuspected consequence of the hor-mone's use was the depletion of the soil; famine fol-lowed overproduction.

But Norvis and Captain Del had swung into action, forming the Merchants' Party, with Del as its leader and Norvis as secretary. By applying pressure on the Council of Elders, the Party forced through corrective agricultural and economic reforms which partially re-stored Nidor's economic balance.

Nidorians, however, were still too used to stability. After the upheaval had begun to die down, the Party began to lose its popular support. Norvis had been driven to do what he had done by his burning hatred for the Earthmen—especially for Smith, who was responsi-ble for ruining Norvis's life—and he felt dissatisfied. He still wanted to drive the Earthmen from Nidor.

And he felt that any means to gain that end was justifiable.

1

There was just one elderly Peaceman guarding the bank that held the wealth of the Province of Dimay. In the cold, rainy drizzle of the Nidorian night, Kris peKym Yorgen paced the deck of his ship, frowning uneasily as he watched the black shadows of his men slipping up on the square-hewn brick building.

Kris peKym turned to the man at his side, a small, wiry Bronze Islander named Dran peDran Gormek. "Is the longboat ready?"

Dran peDran nodded.

"And the deests?"

Again the Bronze Islander nodded.

"Good," Kris said. "The Bank's surrounded. We'll be in possession within three minutes, if all goes well. All we have to do is cut down the one old guard and the keeper—not much protection for millions of weights, is it?"

Dran peDran shook his head. "They isn't expecting any robberies, Captain. You doesn't guard against something you doesn't expect."

Kris smiled. The little outlander's bizarre inflection always amused him—besides, there was truth in what he said. Nidor's Banks were four thousand years old—and in four thousand years, no Bank had ever been robbed. The idea would have been preposterous, once; Nidor's carefully-balanced economy had seen to it that everyone had at least enough for himself, anyway.

Kris' lips curled in a lopsided grin. "There's always a first time, Dran peDran. There was a first time when the Earthmen came, when they first built their School and first started spreading lies and blasphemy among us. And there'll be a first time for robbing the Bank of Dimay." He squinted into the rainy darkness. "Shove off and get into that longboat. They're ready to enter the Bank."

"Right, Captain."

Dran peDran sprang over the side of the deckrail into the waiting longboat below. Oars creaked as he moved off toward the dock. Kris peKym continued to pace the deck anxiously. *First mission for the Party,* he thought. *It has to be perfect.*

He fidgeted, watching the dim silhouette of the Peaceman strolling placidly back and forth before the Bank. The Peaceman was going to be surprised, Kris thought with a grim smile. His family had probably held that sinecure for four thousand years in unbroken succession.

No—no one had ever robbed a Bank before—but it had to be done now. Robbing the Bank would drive a wedge between the people of Nidor and the Earthmen, would leave the Council of Elders in an awkward spot—would, in short, put Nidor one step closer to a return to the old ways.

It was a paradox, thought Kris: in order to return to the old ways, it was necessary to do startlingly new things, like—he chuckled softly—like robbing the

Bank. But the world had changed, in the past century, and further change was needed to return it to the Way of the Ancestors.

He watched as a dark figure edged up quietly behind the unsuspecting Peaceman.

Now, Kris thought. *Now—hit him!*

Kris saw an arm go up, saw the black bulk of a club hover in the air for a moment—and then, travelling quickly and clearly across the water, there came the sound of the club striking the Peaceman's skull. He watched the shadowy form sag to its knees. Two other shadows appeared out of the fog to truss the man thoroughly. So far, so good. The Peaceman would never know what hit him.

Nor would the Keeper of the Bank. Kris smiled as he remembered the man—he had met him three days before, while he and Dran had been making preliminary investigations while ostensibly changing some large coins. The Keeper was a short, rotund man of the Clan Sesom, whose golden body hair had turned nearly silver; he was very fat, and waddled ludicrously around within his Bank.

Straining his ears, Kris thought he heard a grunt from within the Bank. *So much for the Keeper,* he thought.

His men, trained minutely for the job, were carrying the robbery off as if they were so many puppets. Only—

Yes, there it was. The faint clatter of doubly-cleft deest-hooves, behind the Bank. Three of his men were there, mounted. At the signal that the Bank was taken, they were to ride up the marshy back road toward Holy Gelusar for a few miles—far enough for them to take the main-road turn-off, come back, and repeat the whole thing all over again. By the time they had made ten or twelve round trips, it would appear as if a good-sized party of marauders had come down from Gelusar to clean out the Bank.

Meantime, the real unloading was proceeding. The ten men who had entered the vault formed themselves into a human chain stretching from the unseen interior of the Bank to the dock that led from the Bank to the waters of Tammulcor Bay. And then, the cobalt began to move.

It travelled arm-to-arm down the row of men, each heavy loop of coins passing from one to the next, until it reached the dock. The last man was bending and handing the coins through the hole that had been prepared—*I hope those sons of deests didn't hurt those planks*, Kris swore; *I want them to look as good as new when we're done*—and into the longboat that waited under the docks, ready to scuttle through the water under cover of darkness to the *Krand*.

After about fifteen minutes of loading, the chain dispersed. That told Kris that the longboat was full, and that the men were going back to take a breather while the boat was rowed to the *Krand*. Tensely, he listened as the oars creaked in the night, held his breath as the longboat approached.

Then Dran peDran was up on the deck again, looking sweaty and overheated. "We is got the first load, Captain!"

"Fine work," Kris said. "Get it below and go back for more."

"Is going, Captain."

Kris watched as the perspiring crewmen swung the loops of cobalt out of the longboat and onto the deck, where other crewmen grabbed the coins and carried them below to stow them in the false bottom of the

9

Krand. Then the longboat slid silently away in the night, heading back under the dock to receive the next load of coins.

It was long, hard, slow, sweaty work, and it took most of the night. But no one bothered them. Who would be out, late at night, down at the treacherous waterfront? And who would expect the Bank to be robbed, anyway? Such things just didn't happen.

At least they never used to, Kris thought pleasantly.

It was close to morning by the time they were finished. The Bank had been thoroughly robbed, and the money was safely stowed in the ship's false bottom. *The Bank had been robbed.* Strange words, Kris thought—words that never would have been conceived, had the Earthmen never come. But the Earthmen *had* come. It was not yet a hundred years since they had dropped from the skies, claiming to have come from the Great Light Himself. In not a hundred years, Kris thought, the balance of a world had been destroyed.

It was no exaggeration to say that tradition had been demolished and Nidor turned topsy-turvy since the coming of the Earthmen. The Elder Priests of Nidor's Sixteen Clans had accepted them as emissaries from Heaven, had greeted them enthusiastically—and thereby, Kris thought bitterly, had paved the way for their own downfall. Today, the knife and the rifle ruled in a world that had known peace for thousands upon thousands of years—and it was the fault of the Earthmen.

And now, the *Krand* lay innocently at anchor in Tammulcor Bay, its valuable cargo far from sight; it was simply another merchantship resting between voyages.

Kris stood for a while on the deck, while the men

went below. After a few moments, Dran approached hesitantly.

"We is done it, Captain!"

Kris nodded. "Yes, Dran. 'We is done it.' " He paused. "There's no trace of the money?"

"They's never finding it," the Bronze Islander said. "Not without they takes the ship apart."

"Good." Kris stared out over the rain-swept bay at the city sprawling on the mainland. "There'll be fuss and fury in Tammulcor tomorrow," he said wryly. "We'll be able to hear the weeping and wailing from here, when they find out their money's not worth anything any more!"

Dran peDran laughed merrily. "This is good, Captain! We is successful!"

"I hope so." Somehow, Kris found it hard to muster the enthusiasm of his little First Officer, despite the smoothness with which the Bank robbery had been carried out. Only time would tell whether they would be successful in their ultimate goal—the restoration of Nidor. Only time would reveal whether or not the Way of the Ancestors could be attained once again.

Earthmen! Kris thought fiercely and spat into the water of the Bay. *Devils!*

Two weeks before, Kris had been in the eastern seaport of Vashcor, sitting in the office of the Secretary of the Merchants' Party, Norvis peKrin Dmorno, in the Party building—a small stone structure overlooking the sea.

From outside, the raucous cries of the fishmongers and the deep, melodious chanting of sailors killing time on the dock came drifting in, helping to build up a deceptive mood of security—deceptive because there *was* no security to be had on Nidor any longer.

On the walls around the office were posters which showed the intense, brooding face of Party Leader Del peFenn Vyless as reproduced in the blotchy pastels of a cheapjack printer. The Leader was off on a journey to the disturbed area around Elvisen, investigating conditions among the discontented, landless exfarmers clustered in the lowlands there. Kris was glad Del peFenn was elsewhere; he didn't mind dealing with Norvis and the others, but both Kris and Del were strong men and there was inevitably conflict between them—with Del, as the senior member of the organization, invariably coming out ahead.

In the office were two others beside Secretary Norvis. Young Ganz, Del's son, was still a boy, and yet more than a boy, actually a chunky youth with powerful arms and much of Party Leader Del's solid-hewn appearance. His eyes had the same piercing quality as the old sea captain's, and when he spoke his voice was a not dissimilar basso. Unlike his father, he had the quality of keeping his mouth shut when he had nothing to say—but he shared his father's strong anti-priesthood views completely.

Del's daughter, Marja geDel, was, in a way, more like her father than Ganz was. She had the same fiery spirit, the ability to speak her views as she saw them—and—something Del peFenn didn't have—a lush, shimmering beauty about her. Her eyes were deep and wide; the light down that covered her body was a pale, lustrous yellow. She bore herself with Del's erect dignity, but in a feminine way that was oddly pleasing.

At the head of the table sat Norvis peKrin Dmorno, the Secretary of the Party.

Norvis was a quiet man; he seldom said anything except to pass on the orders from Del peFenn. But when he did have something to say, it was important.

He was neither young nor old; he was approaching forty, but the downy hair on his face was still as golden as that of a youth's, and the lines in his face were those of experience, not age. He had been a sea captain, and a good one. Kris could remember when, as a ten-year-old midshipman aboard the *Krand*, he had watched Captain Norvis peKrin give his orders in a quiet, firm voice, commanding obedience but never forcing it. It sometimes seemed odd to Kris that, at that time, Norvis had been little older than he, Kris, was now.

Norvis folded his hands on the table and said: "Here's the position: we—the Party—have been losing ground steadily for nine years. A full Cycle ago, we didn't exist. That means that less than five of our fourteen years of life have actually been productive. During the Great Depression our rolls boomed; today, they're less than—"

Ganz peDel said, "Pardon, Secretary Norvis, but I'm confused. This is the first time I've been at a meeting of the Leader's Advisors, and—"

Norvis' face didn't change. "What troubles you, Ganz peDel?"

"Well, father—uh—our Leader Del peFenn—has told Marja and me something about the Great Depression, but I'm ashamed to say that I never understood it too well. How could *too much* food cause starvation, anyway?"

Marja geDel's smile widened as she turned to Norvis. "Father is a very emotional man; his ideas make sense, but his explanations are sometimes a little limping."

"I understand," Norvis said. "I'll try to explain. Twenty years ago, a hormone was invented by a student at the Bel-rogas School." It was the school that had been established by the Earthmen, nearly a hundred years before. "This hormone was supposed to be a great thing; it was supposed to double the per-acre yield of the peych-bean. The hormone was distributed all over Nidor. And it worked, just as the Earthmen knew it would; twice as many peych-beans were grown that year. We had more of our main crop than we could handle. Everything became worthless—clothes, made from the fiber; paper, made from the pulp; and worst of all, food—made from the fruit of the plant itself.

"The farmers had more than they could eat, but they couldn't sell it—so it never got to the cities. And the big cities starved because no one would bring them a worthless product."

"I see," Ganz said. "And my father—Del pe-Fenn—brought us out of it."

Norvis nodded. "He organized the Merchants' Party and forced the Council of Elders to change its ways. The food was given away to those who needed it. The rest was plowed back into the ground as fertilizer. But until the Party stabilized things, Nidor was in terrible shape. Am I right, Kris?"

Kris nodded grimly.

"Again the Earthmen," Ganz said vindictively. "They've plundered and disturbed Nidor for six cycles—but they've done it through our priesthood. It's the priests who have sold us out to the devils!"

"Easy, Ganz," Norvis said calmly.

Kris frowned. He didn't like such ranting against the priesthood. That was the trouble with Leader Del; he had a habit of alienating the people by preaching against the Elders—and young Ganz was following in his father's steps.

"Just a minute," Norvis said, patting the air with a hand. "We're here to decide on new policy, not to vent our spleens against the Earthmen. If we have anything to say, let's make it constructive."

"Very well then," Marja said. "What's our problem?"

Norvis looked at each of them in turn. "Simply, this: we're in a rut because we haven't had an emergency. During times of trouble, people flock to the Party. When things are relatively easy, we lose members. If we're going to force the Council to return to the Way of the Ancestors, we'll have to have numbers. Therefore—"

"Therefore," Kris said, "We manufacture an emergency."

"Exactly—but how?"

Marja smiled wryly. "We've been going around the same point for weeks, now. We're stuck in a circle."

Norvis cradled his forehead in his hand. "I know. And we're not getting closer to a solution. But what can we do? Use the hormone? No farmer would touch it. Start another hugl plague, as the Earthmen did sixty-odd years ago? There aren't any hugl left, to speak of." He shook his head. "No. Anything I think of is impractical, anyway; we need money to carry them out."

Marja brightened suddenly. "Money? Then why not get it directly?"

"Directly?"

"Of course! Let's go to a Bank and take it!"

To Kris, who had been listening passively, the suggestion came as a jolt. Rob a Bank? Unheard of! But still—

Norvis was nodding. "I like it. By the Great Light, I like it!" He smiled. "Marja, your father would be proud of you! Let's work this out, here and now."

"Who's going to do it?" Kris asked.

15

Marja turned to him, an odd light in her eyes. "I'd say *you're* the best choice," she said. "You've got the ability."

Kris smiled. He'd been thinking along the same lines himself. The job called for a strong man—and if he didn't do it, Del would. "You're right!"

"Okay," said Norvis. "Ganz, you and Marja go out and find me half-a-dozen of the best ship's carpenters in Vashcor. I'll talk to Kris."

"Carpenters? What for?" Ganz said.

"We'll have to make some changes in the *Krand,*" said Norvis. His eyes glittered animatedly. "We'll have to build some sort of secret place, to hide all that money!"

After Marja and Ganz left, Norvis turned to Kris. "It's a tremendous responsibility, Kris peKym." He smiled as if to take the curse off that weighty statement. "I'm sure you can handle it, though."

"I'll do my best," Kris said.

"You'll go to Tammulcor and take the Bank of Dimay. Remember, though, that that territory is dangerous. We've got Vashcor, here, and the Bronze Islands pretty well under control. Sailors are notoriously lax in their religious discipline, anyway—as you well know."

Kris grinned. "I know." As a member of the Clan Yorgen, he could trace his ancestry back to the Great Lawyer, Bel-rogas Yorgen himself—as could a few hundred thousand other Nidorians. Some Yorgens regarded themselves as especially important for this reason—but a few years at sea had robbed Kris peKym of that particular delusion.

"But farmers," Norvis continued, "are different. A farmer depends on his land; he knows that the agriculture of his ancestors was good enough to support a family, and

16

he knows it will support him. The farmer is a simple man; he knows what he needs and he knows how to get it. His life is stable, and that's the way he likes it. Follow?"

Kris nodded. "If a farmer's life becomes unstable because of innovations, the first thing he'll do is scrap the innovations and go back to the old way of doing things. It's almost automatic. The farmer is simple in his outlook."

"Simple, yes," Norvis agreed. "He isn't stupid, though." He stood up, facing Kris, who towered over him by a full head, and stared at the younger man.

"Let me tell you a secret," said Norvis. "You were only a child when the Great Depression hit Nidor. You know who caused that depression?"

"The Earthmen and the Elders," Kris said as if repeating a lesson.

Norvis shook his head. "No," he said. "*I* did. Del peFenn and myself caused that depression."

"*You?*"

Kris felt as though he had been stung. His parents had been sturdy Pelvash farmers. In the Year of the Double Crop, they had been murdered by a band of hungry, marauding scum from the cities. Eight years old, alone and friendless, the orphaned son of old Kym peKinis Yorgen had made his way to Vashcor, to the sea—the only way a young boy could live.

He had signed eight-year papers and been assigned by the Seamen's Guild to the ship of Captain Norvis peKrin Dmorno.

Norvis had come to be almost a father to Kris, teaching him to read and write, filling him with hatred for the Earthmen who were destroying Nidor.

To find that Norvis was partly responsible for the devastation that had caused the Great Depression shocked Kris peKym.

"You were responsible? How?"

"We distributed the hormone to every farmer on Nidor—and so we caused the Collapse." For a moment, a flicker of some unreadable emotion crossed the Secretary's face.

"Why?" Kris asked. "Why did you—"

"Why? It's a complicated story, Kris. Let's just say the Earthmen badly fooled us all. But we managed to cover it up and do our best to straighten things out again."

Kris felt a great flood of relief. How typical of Norvis! Simply because he had been duped by the Earthmen, he was willing to shoulder the responsibility for the whole collapse of the economy.

He smiled at the Secretary. "Well, you *did* straighten things out again."

"Yes—and we took credit for it. But it was the farmer who did the right thing. It was the farmer who saw that the thing to do was to go back to the old way, to quit using the hormone. Of course, we were the ones who told them to plow their rotting crops back into the ground, but the vast majority had already made up their minds to go back to the old way. And the Council of Elders had to go along."

"I follow," Kris said. "With the farmers still persuaded that the Council of Elders knew what it was doing, too. They don't think too clearly, do they?"

"That's not the problem. The thing the farmers cannot seem to see is that our Council of Elders is being misled by the Earthmen. If we don't wake them up, Nidor will be in ruins before another century passes."

"This ought to stir them up. Great Light, what an idea! Robbing a Bank! It's unheard-of!"

Norvis smiled. "Exactly. And that's why it'll work."

"We can certainly use the money," Kris said thoughtfully.

18

"True—but we'll have to use it sparingly. Too much of it dumped on the market at once will cause a panic."

"So? That's just what we need: panic."

"Not that kind. It's—"

Kris looked exasperated. "Look here, stealing the money will cause a panic. Unloading it will cause another. That's what we're looking for—dissatisfaction, unrest, anything to agitate the people against the Earthmen. You've been telling me that ever since I was eight years old."

"Well, yes, of course. But we have to make sure what *kind* of panic. We have to remember what forces are in play." Norvis put his hands together. "The Unit Cobalt Weight is the money of exchange of all Nidor. It has been for four thousand years. For almost as long, the greatest percentage of the actual coin has been kept in the Five Banks of Nidor—one bank in each province. We realized pretty early that a certified piece of paper was just as good as the coin, and, if lost, at least we'd still have the metal. Now what happens if a bank loses most of its metal?"

"I don't have to be lectured to as though I were a child! Come off it, Norvis! Why not a second panic? The first will be nullified as soon as the Council in Gelusar authorizes the amount lost to be coined from the bullion reserves. Why not another panic?"

Norvis shook his head. "I don't think so. We'd lose more than we'd gain. Take a look at it; think it through. What will happen in Dimay if we're successful?"

"Well, bank notes will be worthless—for a while, at least. Then the Council will authorize more coinage, as they always do to make up for coins lost."

"You really think so?"

"Let me finish. These coins *aren't* lost. If we dump all that metal back on the market, the cobalt itself won't be worth as much; we won't have gained anything. We'll have to feed it back into circulation slowly enough to allow the Council to take up the slack by recalling the excess."

"Exactly," Norvis said. "Now, as soon as the ship *Krand* has been rebuilt, you're ready to go."

"How about a crew?"

"That's your job," said Norvis. He smiled. "You're a better leader than I am, Kris peKym—did you know that?"

"I think I am," Kris agreed without conceit. "You're more of a plotter, Norvis peKrin. You can think up beautifully nasty schemes—but you don't know how to handle men."

"Precisely," said Norvis dryly. "That's why Del peFenn Vyless is the leader; I know my limitations. But enough of that. We have to move quickly."

He took Kris peKym's hand. "Good luck, Kris. May the Great Light bring success."

2

Just offshore, two days after the robbery, the schooner
Krand floated peacefully at anchor in the harbor of
Tammulcor. Kris peKym seated himself comfortably in
a chair in his cabin and folded his arms across his broad
chest.

He looked at his First Officer, who squatted cross-
legged on the floor, and his face broke into a broad
grin.

"You don't look worried, Dran peDran."

"I isn't," said the little Bronze Islander. "What does
I has to worry about?"

"Well, we've got eight million weights in cobalt in
the hold of this ship," Kris said nonchalantly. "If the
citizens or the Peacemen of the Province of Dimay ever
find out where it is, you and I will be hanging from the
bowsprit, waiting for the sea-lizards to swoop down and
pick at our corpses."

"Captain," Dran said, "if you is trying to sicken me,
you is not succeeding. As long as you has your life, I is
not worried about mine."

Kris laughed. "We've got them in an uproar, that's
for sure. No one seems to be able to figure out who
stole it or why, or where it went."

21

"They's got priests on the job now, though," Dran said. "I sees five of them around the Bank this afternoon."

"What can they find? Nothing, Dran, nothing."

"We is been here a week, Captain," Dran said. "I is getting nervous."

"If we sailed the day after the robbery," Kris pointed out, "we'd have been first on the list of suspects. As it is, we've got our honest cargo almost loaded, and the long-shoremen have been over every inch of the ship. They'll know—"

He stopped. A voice had sounded over the waters of the Bay of Tammulcor.

"Hoy!" came a faint voice from above. "You—aboard the *Krand!* Hoy!"

Kris peKym cocked his head to one side and listened.

"Hoy, dockboat!" he heard the lookout shout. "What is it?"

"We're special searchers for the Uncle of Public Peace," came the reply. "We'll see your captain!"

Dran shot to his feet. "By my Ancestors!"

Kris lifted his tall, muscular body from the chair, moving like a cat stalking its prey. "Relax, Dran peDran; I can handle this."

He climbed up the ladder to the deck. The torches on the masts shed a flickering orange light over the water, and from above the pale glow of the Lesser Light shining through the eternal clouds gave a ghostly monochromatic background to the circle of orange.

Kris walked to the port bulwark and looked over the side. A dinghy with five men in it was pulling up to the ladder.

"I'm captain here," Kris told them. "What's your business?"

"Special searchers for the Uncle of Public Peace," the leader repeated.

Kris frowned. "Looking for what?" he asked sharply. "We have no criminals aboard."

"That's to be seen," the Peaceman said. "We're not looking for men anyway; we're looking for cobalt."

"For what? Now, look here—I've paid my harbor fee."

"We'll take none that's legally yours. Let us aboard."

Kris shrugged and signalled the deckman. "Lower the ladder."

As the five Peacemen came aboard, Kris just stood there, his balled fists on his hips, looking at them coldly. Several crewmen stood about, fingering handy belaying pins. The crew of the *Krand* was a tight, cohesive unit that stood firmly behind Kris.

"You're Captain Kris peKym Yorgen?" the official asked. "Commanding the *Krand,* out of Vashcor?"

"I am," Kris said coldly. "And now that you're aboard my vessel, you'd better prove you are who you say—or the sea-things will eat tonight."

It was the right thing to say, Kris knew. The other sea captains would be equally suspicious of anyone who came aboard their vessels. In the first place, Peacemen had no right to interfere in honest trade; in the second place, these might not be Peacemen in the first place.

The mob violence which had threatened Tammulcor and all of the Province of Dimay in the past several days made one suspicious of anyone and everyone.

The Peacemen fingered the heavy truncheons at their belts while their leader took a neatly-folded paper from his sash pouch. He handed it to Kris, who opened it and read the order from the Uncle of Public Peace.

He smiled and looked up. "Stolen cobalt, eh? What happened?" His voice was no longer truculent, and hands dropped from truncheons.

23

"Hadn't you heard that the Bank of Dimay was robbed?" the leader asked.

"I had heard, yes," Kris said casually. "But not the details."

"One hundred manweights of cobalt were taken. A group of men struck the Keeper of the Bank and took the money away. It was a most evil sin, and most incomprehensible."

Kris nodded. "True. What would anyone want with so much money? And why do you come to me?"

"The money must have been taken away somehow. It may be aboard a ship. We have to search every ship that comes into the harbor. You see that we—"

"I see," Kris said. He turned to his first officer. "Dran peDran, show these men through the ship. Eight million weights of cobalt coin could not be hidden easily."

No indeed, Kris was thinking. *It's hard to hide thirty-six cubic feet of metal. Especially when it's in the form of coin.*

While Dran led the police below, Kris climbed to the bridge and leaned against the mainmast, watching the shore. The seconds passed slowly, and he found himself listening keenly to the sounds of the harbor—the creaking of a distant oar, the soft, unvarying lapping of the waves against the side of the ship, the sounds of men chanting far away on the shore or on some hauling-vessel entering the harbor.

The next few minutes would mean the success or failure of the voyage, Kris thought. And a failure here, at this time, might mean the failure of the whole Merchants' Party.

Kris smiled grimly. He'd staked his life with the Merchants—with Leader Del peFenn and with Secretary Norvis. It just wouldn't do to have the whole thing blow up in their faces right now, with Nidor still in the grip of the misguided Elders and the devil Earthmen hovering ambiguously in the background.

And now Captain Kris peKym stood on the deck of his ship, waiting for success—or failure. If the police found the secret of the double hull in the bilge of the ship, the whole project would collapse right there. It would do no good in the long run to kill the five investigators—though that would have to be done, of course. But the Uncle of Public Peace would know what had happened, and, within a day, Kris peKym Yorgen and his crew would be hunted men.

He waited patiently. There was no noise from below as yet. His men would come down on the hapless five with belaying pins just as soon as the fatal discovery was made—*if* it was made, that is. He steeled himself and waited for the outcome.

It took a while before the constables reappeared. They were trained searchers, and they had done a thorough job, having searched through the vessel for nearly three hours. When they came above, though, it was immediately apparent to Kris that they had been unsuccessful.

He smiled to himself. Obviously, they didn't even as much as suspect the existence of a false hold in the bottom of the ship. After all, a ship is only built one way; the thought that anyone might break time-honored tradition would never enter into their heads.

The leader of the squad seemed a great deal more at ease than he had been when he had boarded the ship. "Well?" Kris asked. "Find the untold millions below?"

"I'm glad to say your ship's in fine order, Captain. Not a trace of contraband of any sort. But still—"

"Yes?" Kris asked suspiciously.

"It's very odd, you know. A hundred manweights of cobalt is no easy load; how could it disappear like that? It's like magic."

Kris looked thoughtfully at the top of the mizzenmast. "Yes. You're right. It's almost as though the stuff had floated off into thin air—as the Earthmen do, when they leave us."

A startled expression crossed the constable's face. "You aren't suggesting—"

"Oh, no!" Kris said, his face taking on an expression of horror. "Great Light forbid! No! But, as you said, it looks like magic."

The officer scowled. "Little help that is. Well, that'll be all. Good sailing, Captain Kris peKym."

Without another word, he and his men climbed down to the dinghy and rowed off. Kris barely managed to repress the urge to chuckle as their oars swept busily through the water.

When they were a good distance from the ship, Kris breathed deeply and turned around to Dran peDran.

"All right, let's turn in. We have to take sail tomorrow—and we have to look like honest sailors, don't we?"

Then he noticed the peculiarly solemn look on the First Officer's face.

"What's the matter, Dran peDran?"

The little Bronze Islander glanced apprehensively at the Public Peace dinghy that was moving smoothly away, some hundred yards from the ship. "We is got somewhat of trouble, Captain. Come below, eh?"

Kris followed Dran down the ladder to the First Officer's cabin. There, he saw two burly sailors standing guard over a third seaman. The prisoner looked dazed.

"We has to clout him on the head when we find what

he is up to, Captain. Look at this." He handed Kris a bit of paper.

Kris took the words scribbled on it in at a quick glance:

The money is in a false bottom built into the ship. I had nothing to do with the robbery. Ask the Grandfathers to pray for me.

It was signed, *Vels peKorvin Danoy.*

"He is trying to give it to the Peaceman when I catch him," said Dran peDran.

Kris frowned. "Did you write this, Vels peKorvin?"

"Sure he write it!" Dran snarled. "I signal the boys when I see him, and they clout him and take him here! We tell the Peacemen that he is seasick," he added as an afterthought.

"Quiet, Dran," Kris said softly. "Let *him* talk. Did you write this, Vels peKorvin?"

The prisoner looked up stiffly. "I wrote it, Captain. To steal money from a bank is nothing but sacrilege. It is a sin which I do not want on my soul."

"Why didn't you just denounce us?" Kris asked. His voice was still soft.

"It would have done no good," Vels said bitterly. "You would have killed us all. But if they got the note, they could have done something about it later, after they got ashore."

"Then you admit your guilt? You admit you have endangered the life of those aboard this vessel?" Kris crossed his arms sternly. "There is only one sentence for that, Vels peKorvin Danoy."

"I know. But I did what I thought was right."

"Very well." Kris turned to Dran. "Prepare a Cup of Eternal Quiet."

The little First Officer registered astonishment. "What, Captain? The drug is only for those who is too

27

badly hurt to live, or for those who is dying of an evil growth! Traitors is hanged!"

"Quiet!" Kris said sharply. "Hanging is for criminals; stoning is for blasphemers. Vels peKorvin is neither. He has done what he thought was right. If he had done it through fear of being caught, if he had denied it through cowardice, if he had tried to smuggle the Peacemen the note because of his fear of us—then I most assuredly would have hanged him. But he did what he did because of a mistaken belief that we are not on the side of the Great Light; he thinks that following the way of the Earthmen is following the Way of our Ancestors. Therefore, his death shall be honorable. Bring the Cup, Dran peDran."

The First Officer bobbed his head. "Yes, sir. I sees." He turned quickly and left the room.

Kris faced the stony-featured prisoner. "Your clan, the Danoy, will be told that you died in the course of duty, Vels peKorvin. I will see that the Passing Service is said for you at the Temple in Vashcor."

Hypocrite! Kris thought accusingly. *All this solemnity when the thing to do is just to heave the man overboard. But revolutions move slowly.*

The seaman bowed his head. "You are a great man, Captain, even though you are misled. My prayers shall be for you."

"And mine for you. Would you care to hear the Scripture?"

The sailor nodded.

Kris crossed the tiny cabin to the locker where Dran peDran kept his personal belongings. He opened it, took out a thick book bound in brown deest-leather, and began leafing through it.

At that moment, Dran peDran came in quietly, holding a cup of peych beer. The little cabin was silent as the prisoner took the bitter-tasting cup and drank it. He lay down on the bunk, face down, his hands clasped above his head. It would be a few minutes before the poison took effect.

"The Book of History," Kris peKym said. "Eighth section. 'And the Great Light spoke to the Lawyer Belrogas, saying: the Cataclysm has destroyed those who were not righteous, and they shall suffer forever. But he who dies for My sake shall live in eternal peace.

'Now, at that time, a certain man came to Belrogas . . .'"

3

The *Krand* weighed anchor at firstlight, sailing out of
the Bay of Tammulcor and making her way due east,
along the coast. She skirted Thyvocor, the small port
city of Thyvash Province, staying well out to sea so that
her tall masts would not bc seen. Then she angled
northeast, heading for the Bronze Islands.

The trip was uneventful. The *Krand* dropped anchor
well offshore in the dead of night. In the distance could
be heard the rumble of the sea splashing against tall
cliffs, and the occasional cry of a flying sea-lizard.

Silently and carefully the crew set to work. All that
night they labored, doing their job doggedly and without cease. A ship's longboat made the passage from
ship to shore and back again many times. It was not
until firstlight that Kris announced that the job was
nearly done. He made the last trip himself.

Kris peKym eased himself down into the longboat
and whispered: "Dran peDran, if you make those oars
creak one more time, I swear I'll tie a rock around your
neck and throw you overboard."

"Us is made twelve trips in this boat," said Dran
stolidly. "Us is carried lots heavier cargoes than you is,

Captain. How many creaks is you heard?"

Kris glanced at the other crewmen in the dim illumination of the setting Lesser Light. "I heard three," he said succinctly. "And that's about four too many."

One of the men chuckled a little as he pulled at the oars, and Dran's sharp whisper cut across the merriment. "You doesn't laugh at the Captain's jokes at a time like this! Shut quiet!"

Kris grinned in the darkness as the longboat moved toward the shore in the blackness. They were a good crew; they knew what they were doing, and they knew how to keep their mouths shut. And they were loyal; that was the one important thing. They knew that their captain was right, and they'd follow him to the Rim of the World itself.

The *Krand* was anchored off the rocky shore of Bellinet, the largest of the Bronze Islands. Nearby was a small village. None of these villagers must know that the great load of cobalt from the *Krand's* false hull was being unloaded here.

The constant drizzle of rain that marked every Nidorian night wetted the bodies of the sweating seamen and dripped gently into the bottom of the boat. And there, the heavy cobalt coins glistened metallically in the faint light. It was the last load; the rest of the loot from the Bank of Dimay already lay in the tidal cave beneath the cliff.

After several minutes, Dran peDran whispered: "Captain! Us is here. Does you want to go in?"

Kris nodded. "I'll help you transfer it inside. We've got to hurry." He glanced up and frowned. The rain was already letting up; soon, the Great Light would be coloring the eastern sky.

He and the crewmen stripped off their black seamen's uniforms—a vest and knee-length trousers, all alike except for the white stripes on the front of the vests of the officers.

Kris slid silently into the gently heaving water, feeling it cool against his overheated body. "All right, Dran," he whispered harshly. "Give me the first load."

Dran heaved a string of coins out of the bottom of the boat. Each coin was pierced by the symbolic triangular hole which stood for the beam of light that pierced the lens of each temple as it illumined the altar. Through each of the holes ran a strong bronze wire, which was twisted to form a loop. And on each loop was a quarter of a manweight in coins—more than twenty thousand manweights of solid cobalt!

Kris grasped a loop in each hand, took a deep breath, and dropped to the sandy bottom of the surging sea, twenty feet below the surface. Slowly pushing his way toward the cliff ahead, he felt his way with his feet. As long as he kept on the sand, he was all right.

In the darkness, it was difficult to tell where he was going, but the gentle slope of coral sand that spilled out of the underwater cave before him was easy to follow. He moved one foot after another cautiously.

Holding the loops of coins, he pushed himself toward the cliff. Finally, he felt the opening in the wall. He lowered his head and crept up the slope toward the cave beneath the cliff. The only opening was completely underwater at all times, and travelling the passage, especially with a heavy load, required the ability to hold a breath and keep from panicking.

When at last his head broke water, Kris peKym took a deep, gasping breath. Above him, in the cave, were two of his crewmen. One of them held out a hand.

"I'll take the coin, Captain."

Kris handed the two loops up to him. The light of the

flickering oil lamp cast changing, moving shadows across the interior of the dark cavern.

Kris climbed up from the pool that led to the outside and walked with the two men who were carrying the loops. They went to the heavy, leaden casket at the far end of the cave. It was filled with oil, the sea-smelling oil of the great lizards that prowled the coasts of the Bronze Islands. The huge, vegetarian beasts were excellent sources of oil, although it was scarcely worthwhile to ship it to the mainland of Nidor, where plant oils from the ubiquitous peych-bean were so cheap.

The coins went into the oil-filled chest. In sea-water, even cobalt would pit and deteriorate. The oil would protect it for a while.

Kris watched as the rest of the boatload, representing the last of the great mass of cobalt that had been taken from the Bank of Dimay, was hauled, loop by loop, into the hidden cavern.

When the last one had been dumped into the chest, he grinned and said, "That's the last of it, boys. She'll stay there until we need her. Lock it up."

One of the seamen stepped up to the casket, closed the lid, and padlocked it. He handed the heavy bronze key to Kris. "There he is, Captain," he said, a twisted smile crossing his face. "They'll never find it here."

There was one more precaution. They shoveled sand and heavy chunks of coral over the box, covering it completely. When that was done, Kris said, "All's well, boys. Let's go."

The cobalt was buried now—the cobalt whose theft could trigger the movement that would, at last, drive the hated Earthmen from Nidor. Kris hoped so.

He took one last look. Then the three of them dived into the pool and swam through the passage to the waiting longboat.

The Great Light was just beginning to lighten the cloudladen sky in the east.

In Vashcor, that same day, Norvis peKrin Dmorno and Marja geDel Vyless were performing their duties at the Party headquarters with more than usual energy.

"So Kris has succeeded in robbing the Bank," Marja said. "Wonderful!"

"It is," the Secretary said quietly. "He carried the job off perfectly—and your father's out in the towns now, making speeches claiming it was the Elders who did it."

"Will that line of approach work?"

"I'm not sure," Norvis said. "It's your father's policy, though, and he's the Leader. For fourteen years, Del's been preaching against the Council. If he keeps it up, he may eventually convince the people that the Elders *are* corrupt."

"Where's Kris now?" Marja asked.

"Caching the money, no doubt. He ought to be back here soon. Why?"

"Oh—nothing much, Norvis. It's—just that I'd like to see him again. It's kind of comforting, having a big man like Kris around the office."

Norvis smiled wryly. "Thanks, Marja."

"I didn't mean—"

"I understand."

"I know you do. Kris is—well, sort of wonderful. I wish I could get to know him better. But he's always out crusading someplace or other, just like Father."

"Maybe you'll get the chance soon, Marja. If—"

He was interrupted by a sound of knocking at the door.

"Come in!"

A yellow-clad acolyte entered. "From the Priest-

Mayor," he mumbled. "A message." He handed Norvis a sealed envelope, which the Secretary broke open immediately and read.

"What is it, Norvis?"

"Grandfather Marn peFulda wants to see me at once. I'd better go, I guess."

"Norvis peKrin Dmorno, Secretary to the Merchants' Party," the acolyte intoned.

Grandfather Marn peFulda Brajjyd, Priest-Mayor of Vashcor, looked up as Norvis entered the office. "The peace of your ancestors be with you always," he said.

"May the Great Light illumine your mind as he does the world."

"Sit down, my son. We'll not stand on ceremony here."

As Norvis sat, the Grandfather lifted an eyebrow at the acolyte who stood at the door. "Be about your duties," he said. "I have nothing to fear from Norvis peKrin Dmorno."

The acolyte bowed and left, but it seemed to Norvis that there was a trace of reluctance in his demeanor.

"My staff is rather on edge," the Grandfather explained apologetically. "They seem to fear for my life."

"They have nothing to fear from me, Ancient One," Norvis said.

"I know. But the priesthood is not exactly in good odor here in Vashcor; my Mayoralty is hardly considered any more."

Norvis shrugged. "For that, Aged Grandfather, I am sorry."

"I know." Suddenly, the priest put his finger to his lips and winked. "I'd like to have you take a look at this," he said.

He rose and tiptoed to the door, his blue robes gathered up with one hand so they wouldn't rustle. He winked again.

Norvis caught the meaning of the gesture and said, "Very interesting, Grandfather. Very interesting. May I look at it again?"

The priest paused at the door for a moment, then jerked it open suddenly. The acolyte who had been listening at the hinge crack nearly fell inward. He regained his balance just in time, after a half-stagger, and his golden facial hair was suffused with a pink glow of embarrassment from beneath.

"You were told to go about your duties, Gyls peDorf," the priest said sternly. "You disobeyed."

"Yes, Grandfather." The acolyte shrank in on himself in an agony of humiliation. *An unsuccessful eavesdropper,* Norvis reflected, *is a pitiful sight.*

"Having disobeyed my order, you must take your punishment. Go to your cell; fast and pray for the next three days. Go, Gyls peDorf."

The acolyte took off down the hall as though all the demons of the Outer Darkness were after him—which, of course, might well have been the case.

Chuckling to himself, the Grandfather closed the door again and returned to his desk. "Thank you, my son; you have a quick wit. My staff is loyal—too loyal, sometimes, I fear. But no one will hear us now."

Norvis gave the priest a half-smile. The cleric had something on his mind; that much was obvious.

"My son," the old man began, "it is more than fourteen years since a man has been stoned for blasphemy on Nidor. Before that, no man had been punished thus for over two centuries. You may recall the case. It took place in Holy Gelusar itself, and the man stoned was Norvis peRahn Brajjyd, the grandson of Grandfather Kiv peGanz Brajjyd, the present leader of the Council of Elders."

"I recall," Norvis said, trying to keep his voice calm. Did the priest know? Did he know that the man he was talking to was that very Norvis peRahn Brajjyd, the boy who presumably had been stoned to death the year before the Great Depression began?

"Before that instance," the Grandfather went on implacably, "no one had been stoned because there was no blasphemy—or, at least, none in public. There has been no one stoned since because blasphemy has become almost commonplace. We live in wicked times, my son."

"I quite agree, Grandfather."

Grandfather Marn peFulda said: "We have a problem here, Norvis peKrin. I'll put it bluntly. The Leader of your Merchants' Party—Del peFenn Vyless—is a troublemaker. Ever since the robbery of the Bank of Dimay, he has been implying that we—the priesthood—are behind it."

"You must forgive Del, Grandfather," Norvis said quickly. "He preaches against the Council of Elders, true—but remember, he *is* a sailor, and seamen are likely to become acerbic at times."

Marn peFulda shook his head. "That's not the point, my son. I don't disagree with what you have to say. I, too, think that the Earthmen are—ah—a disturbing influence on Nidorian culture. I would—ahem—like to see any such influences removed. But I don't think destroying our Government is the way to do it."

Norvis felt a slight shock. The thought that any of the priesthood would agree with the Merchants' Party program, would have any point of tangency whatsoever, was, to say the least, unusual.

He leaned back in his chair, stroking the downy fuzz

37

on his cheek. "I don't think I quite follow you, Grandfather."

The Priest-Mayor looked worried and thoughtful. His face seemed somehow gaunt, and the silver of his facial hair looked oddly gray. Moving slowly, deliberately, he leaned across his desk toward Norvis. When he spoke, his voice was low, almost a whisper.

"I want to tell you something, my son. I don't want you to interrupt, because, if you do, I may not be able to finish what I have to say. I will speak to you as though we were of the same age, as though there were no difference between us. Forget that I am a priest; remember only that I am a Nidorian."

Norvis nodded. "I will listen, Marn peFulda."

He had not used the formal manner of address, and the priest looked just a trifle surprised for a second. Then he smiled bleakly.

"Thank you, Norvis peKrin. I know that what I say will not go beyond you—but if it does, I will refute it."

"You need have no fear, Marn peFulda." For the second time, Norvis used the familiar address.

"Very well, then. And, as I said, no interruptions." He paused. "The Council of Elders is blind. When the Great Light told us our duties, immediately after the Cataclysm, he spoke through the great Lawyer Bel-rogas." Marn peFulda tapped the Book of Scripture on his desk. "It is all here, and we cannot disbelieve His Word. But Bel-rogas warned us that the Great Light had also spoken of the Great Darkness."

Norvis said nothing. The mention of the Great Darkness was well known, but no one paid any attention to it any more. Norvis, whose theological studies at the Bel-rogas School of Divine Law had been abruptly interrupted, two decades before, by a trumped-up expulsion arranged by the Earthmen, had little love for theology in any event.

"The Great Darkness, according to Bel-rogas, is the antithesis of the Great Light," the Grandfather said. "It is a being whom the Great Light created as a counterbalance to Himself.

"Of late, we have come to discount the power of the Great Darkness. We have come to think of him as merely a natural phenomenon, as an absence of the Great Light. Through four thousand years of history, we have seen that when night comes there is nothing to fear. The Great Light is not shining upon us at night, but we do not find in darkness a negation of light, merely the absence of light.

"But I tell you that the Great Darkness is a *living being,* as alive and ambitious as you or I! Through forty centuries, he has remained silent, not obtruding himself upon us, waiting until we no longer believed in *him* as a personality. And now, his time has come. He is here, among us; he has sent his minions to corrupt our priesthood, our Council, our lives, and the Way of our Ancestors.

"We of Nidor have travelled in the right path, we have moved in the Way of the Light. Why? Because we dared not follow the Darker Path? No. We moved in the Way of the Light because we knew no other way. The Great Darkness had not tempted us with that Way. But now—now we have been invited to try the path of Darkness." He paused again and looked questioningly at Norvis. "How do you feel about this?"

"You may be right, Grandfa—Marn peFulda. But how do we know that one Path is better than the other?"

The priest looked scornful. "Is it better to walk in the light of day, where one can see where one is going, where one can see one's goal, or is it better to walk during the night, when one cannot see what lies ahead of him, when his goal is obscured in blackness?"

Norvis shifted uncomfortably in his seat. He could see what argument the Grandfather was driving toward, but he wasn't quite sure he wanted to agree with it on theological grounds. "Where are you heading, Grandfa— Marn peFulda?"

"Just this: it is obvious from the history of the past century that we have been diverted from the Way of our Ancestors. And I say that it is the Earthmen who have done this! The Earthmen who came among us and built their School, up in Holy Gelusar, supposedly to teach the Law. A stream of wickedness has come from the School under the guise of Light. The School has changed our world—taking our best minds, twisting them, filling them with words of the Earthmen. The Earthmen are the minions of the Great Darkness!"

Norvis frowned. He had much the same opinion of the Earthman-founded Bel-rogas School, but he had scarcely expected to hear it from a priest. *Marn must not have gone to the School,* he thought.

To test the priest's logic he asked, "But Grandfather—the Earthmen walk and act and speak in the daylight, when the Great Light shines. How can that be?"

"Can't you see, my son? The Scripture is metaphorical in its meaning. The passages are symbolical. They do not mean the darkness of an ordinary night; they mean the Darkness of a lack of morality, the Darkness of a rejection of the Way of our Ancestors, the Darkness of the deviation from the Path of the Great Light."

"I think I follow you, Grandfather. In fact, I'm sure I do." He paused for a moment. These were surprising words to hear from a priest's lips—and evidently it was an opinion the priest had been nursing a long time.

"My position," said Grandfather Marn peFulda, "is this: I believe that the Earthmen are agents of the

Great Darkness—in fact, I *know* them to be so. But I cannot condone the attitude of Del peFenn Vyless, the Leader of your party."

That's no surprise, Norvis thought. *The way Del howls for the heads of the Elders, it's a wonder the good Grandfather can keep a civil tongue in his head when he speaks of him.*

"I do not feel," the priest went on, "that the proper service of the Great Light includes the throwing-over of His ordained priesthood; it must include only the correction of the evils which have invaded the Council of Elders. And if you were to change the line of attack of your Party somewhat, I—I might be persuaded to lend some influence of my own."

A reformer! Norvis thought. He could hardly keep from smiling. It was exactly what he wanted—exactly what the Party needed! He had hardly dared hope it would happen.

Priest against priest; liberal orthodoxy against reactionary reformation—nothing could be more suited to his plans.

"Very well, Grandfather," he said. "I'll see what can be done." This interview altered things considerably. He had to leave, now. He wanted to send an anonymous note to Grandfather Kiv, the head of the Council—pitchforking Kiv into action that would set in motion the climax of the plan.

The priest nodded solemnly and raised his crossed forearms in benediction. "May the Great Light illumine your mind, my son, and lead you to the Way of Light."

"May He illumine your mind as He does the world," said Norvis, bowing.

4

In his office in Holy Gelusar, capital city of Nidor, Elder Grandfather Kiv peGanz Brajjyd—leader of the Council of Elders of the Sixteen Clans, and traditionally the most powerful man on Nidor—sat quietly, staring at the sheet of printed lettering on the desk before him.

He winced, glanced away. In order to dismiss it from his mind for the moment, Grandfather Kiv peGanz lifted his eyes to the window which looked out on the Holy City. There were buildings out there, buildings which had stood for centuries. Some of them had stood for two, perhaps three thousand years.

Gelusar, the City of the Great Light Himself, seemed safe from the corruption of the masses, but—

But *was* it? Was it *really* safe?

Again he glanced at the note, as though to discover some meaning which was different from the meaning he had read before. No new interpretation came, though. There was none. The words remained the same.

Grandfather Kiv glanced reflectively up at the cloudladen sky for a moment. Then, leaving the note on his desk, he locked his office and went down to the Temple. He knew he couldn't carry the weight of this decision alone.

The dim vault of the Temple was empty except for a few worshippers here and there, praying among the kneeling benches.

There were less than usual, Kiv noticed, as he made his way down the aisle toward the altar. It had not been like that when he was younger. He could remember long ago, when the Earthmen had first come, the days when the Temple had been steamy with the breath of many worshippers.

He remembered the Hugl Crisis—a crisis that he, himself had caused, more than fifty years before. The people had flocked to the Temples then.

Kiv sighed deeply. His seven decades of life weighed heavily upon him. His daughter, Sindi, had died, miserable and unhappy. His only grandson, Norvis peRahn, had been stoned to death for blasphemy, more than fourteen years before.

He lifted his eyes toward the altar. From the great lens in the roof of the temple, the diffuse rays of the Great Light were focussed upon the refracting surface of the stone altar top.

Great Light, he asked, *what have I done?*

The focus of the Great Light was near the Left Pit. Kiv knelt before the glowing spot, keeping his eyes carefully averted.

O Great Light, he asked again, *what have I done?*

And this time, he seemed to hear a voice. *What have you done? Nothing!*

For a moment, Kiv peGanz felt deep relief.

And then the full import of what he had seemed to hear struck him.

Nothing?

Had he done *nothing?*

Had he neglected to do what he ought to have done?

He glanced at the Pit in which the Great Light

seemed to burn. It seared his eyes and he turned away. What was it the Earthman, Jones, had called the Great Light?

A blue-white star.

What it meant, Kiv had no notion, but he had been told it by the blessed Earthman more than five decades before.

For the first time, he raised his eyes to the lens in the roof. And he made a prayer that had never been heard before on Nidor.

'O, Great and Holy Bluewhitestar," he said softly, "if I have not acted according to Your wishes, if I have not acted at all—then give me the strength to act now."

He paused for a moment, but there was no response.

"I thank you, O Great Light. You have illumined my mind."

Rising quickly, he genuflected and then hastened toward his office. The other worshippers seemed to pay no attention to the old man's coming and going.

Back at his office, he looked once again at the note. *I have done nothing,* he thought. *I must act.*

The note said:

> *Most Holy and Ancient Grandfather:*
> *It has come to my attention that a certain thief has stolen eight million weights of cobalt from the Bank of Dimay. According to the Law, the vaults of the Holy City of Gelusar must make up any losses of money. But if you do this, and the extra money which has been stolen is spent by the thieves, it will lower the value of all our money.*
> *On the other hand, if you do not replace it, the Bank of Dimay will fail.*
> *What is your decision, Ancient Grandfather?*

The note was unsigned.

Kiv fingered it for a moment. *Can I take the chance?* he asked himself.

No. He couldn't. He had to assume that the note was true. If he replaced the coinage in the vaults of the Bank of Dimay, then, when the thief dumped all that coinage on Nidor, every weight would be devalued. Money would be worthless.

Yet, if he refused to replace the money, the Bank of Dimay would be bankrupt, and its scrip mere paper. But the rest of Nidor would maintain its monetary integrity.

That was the core of the matter. It was the Bank of Dimay against all of Nidor—and Dimay would have to be sacrificed. Whether the note were true or not, there was only one thing he could do. And, by the Great Light, he *would* do it!

Calmly, the old priest reached for the pen on his desk. His gnarled hands quivered a little, but he pulled a sheet of embossed paper to him and began to write.

The *Krand* made its way into the crowded harbor of Vashcor nearly a week later, with Kris peKym standing proudly on the deck, staring at the sprawling seaport as if he were about to receive a hero's ovation.

They docked at one of the smaller piers, and Kris turned to Dran peDran. "When the cargo is unloaded, give the men a day's liberty," he told the Bronze Islander. "I'm going to pay a visit to Headquarters to see what our next job is."

"Is fine, sir," Dran peDran said.

Kris nodded and climbed ashore. He moved quickly through the knot of sailors and dockhands that thronged the busy waterfront, heading toward the small frame house that was the headquarters of the Merchants' Party.

Norvis peKrin Dmorno looked up and smiled in greeting as Kris entered.

"Well! The pirate has returned!"

"Safe and sound," Kris said, glancing around. "I see Del is not back yet."

"No," Norvis said. "I expected him back yesterday, but there's been so much trouble in Tammulcor that he must have been delayed. How did your voyage go?"

"Well enough. We brought back copper and tin from the Bronze Islands, and cloth from Tammulcor." He frowned, then added: "And we lost a man: Vels peKorvin Danoy. He went overboard during the voyage." Kris saw no need to elaborate; the affair was closed, and such losses at sea were not uncommon.

Norvis nodded. "I'll see that the proper papers are filed. Have you heard the news about Tammulcor? There's trouble down there."

"I dare say," Kris replied, grinning. "What happened? Someone rob a Bank?"

Norvis was only slightly amused. "That, and more. The Council, under instruction from Elder Grandfather Kiv peGanz Brajjyd, has refused to replace the money. The scrip of Dimay is utterly worthless."

Kris looked puzzled. "Why the devil did he do that?"

Norvis smiled. "Because he doesn't know where the cobalt is, of course. If he were to replace it, and back the Bank of Dimay, what would happen if we dumped all that cobalt back on the market? There would be eight million weights too many floating around Nidor. See?"

Kris nodded. "Good. When are we going to dump it then? You want me to go back and dig the stuff up?"

"Not at all. It's causing more than enough trouble right where it is." The Secretary leaned backward and put his hands behind his head. "We're *wicked*, aren't we?" he asked suddenly.

"Living devils," said Kris. He stood there silent for a moment, toying with a carved-ivory statuette some sailor had made from a bone of a large sea animal and had given to Secretary Norvis long ago.

Suddenly, the abrupt *plop plop plop* of cloven deest-hooves sounded outside. Kris looked up to see Leader Del pulling up at the hitching-post in front of Headquarters.

Kris nodded coolly as the Leader entered. Del's fine golden body-down was covered with a dull coating of roaddust from his journey, and he showed signs of fatigue.

"Miserable trip," Del peFenn Vyless grunted as he strode in and sat down. "I'd rather sail from Gycor to Lidacor the long way than travel from Tammulcor by deest."

"How come you rode?" Kris asked.

"Couldn't get a ship," said Del. "I was in Elvisen when I found out there was trouble down in the south, so I rode down there. But the harbor's so fouled up because of the riots that there weren't any passenger ships available." He coughed and wiped perspiration from his face.

"Find out anything interesting down there?" Norvis asked.

"Aye," Del peFenn said heavily. He was a big man, tall for a Nidorian, with wide, muscular shoulders. He still walked with the rolling stride of a seafaring man, although it had been ten years since he had last captained a merchantship. "Aye. We have a bunch of raggle-tail grumblers who don't know what they want but who know they don't like things the way they are."

"Sounds like promising material for us," Kris said.

Del dropped into a chair at the side of the bare room. "I don't know," he said. "The fatheads didn't want to listen to me."

At Del's bitter words, Kris felt a moment of triumph. He *knew* blustering, clumsy Del was doing things the wrong way—and here the Leader himself was admitting failure!

Del shook his head. "The Elders pulled the rug out from under those people by scragging their bank. They're rioting, marching up and down, burning things and yelling. And yet—yet they can't be persuaded that the priests are no good for them. I don't understand it, Norvis."

"Suppose we send Kris down there?" Norvis suggested suddenly. "We need Tammulcor—it's the lifeline of Gelusar and all the Central Plains area. It's a trading port surrounded by plenty of farming country—and the farmers are still on the side of the Elders, despite all that's happened to them."

"Why send Kris?" Del asked uneasily.

"He's a new face. He might be able to do the trick where you failed. They know you from way back, and they know you don't respect their religion. They *don't* know Kris."

Del considered that for a moment. "All right," he said finally. "Let's send Kris to Tammulcor." He turned to face Kris peKym, who had been watching the interplay silently and without opinion. "You better go by deest," he said. "The harbor's blocked up."

"You want me to go immediately?" Kris asked, surprised despite himself.

Del nodded. "I think so. Come—let's sit down and plan out what you're going to say to them."

5

Oh, the life for me is the heaving sea,
And the feel of a keel afloat;
The rise and dip of a sturdy ship
Or the roll of a rocking boat!

Kris peKym's strong baritone rang joyously through the warm, humid summer air.

"You is so right, Captain," Dran peDran said. His voice sounded tired. "My tail is weary from the back of this cursed deest. It's no way for an honest sailor to travel."

"Quiet, youngster," Kris said smilingly. "The feel of a deest ride, if you but had the sense to notice it, is very like that of a boat."

"Yes. I is in agreement. I is never been sea-sick in my life, but I is definitely deest-sick now."

Kris grinned. "Better get used to the swing of it, Dran. We've got a long way to go."

The seaport of Thyvocor was not far behind them; Tammulcor was more than a day's journey overland ahead. They were on the second leg of their journey southwest to the big seaport. There was a direct route from Vashcor to Tammulcor, but it was winding, dusty, and rarely travelled. There was the constant menace of bandits to be considered, too. Instead of the overland route, Kris and Dran peDran had taken the coastal packet south from Vashcor to Thyvocor, and there had purchased two sturdy-looking deests with which to complete the journey overland from midpoint. Vashcor lay directly west of the small port of Thyvocor.

"Flat, dull country this is," Dran commented as they spurred their mounts through the coastal lowlands.

Kris nodded. It *was* dull country, all marshy gray-green grass and flat, swampy plain. But it was necessary to cross through it, and so they *were* crossing it. It sometimes was necessary, Kris realized, to do perfectly dull, dreary things like crossing the lowlands, in order to get to where more exciting things could happen.

Like getting to Tammulcor, for instance—Tammulcor, where bewildered men were rioting and demonstrating against anything and everything. Once in Tammulcor, Kris would face a difficult job, but he was looking forward to it.

There was an analogy. For the past three years, he had taken orders from Del peFenn—dull, blockheaded, blustering Del peFenn. Kris had threatened rebellion from time to time, but Norvis had always managed to smooth things over. Now, at last, Del peFenn had sent Kris off to Tammulcor in a position of unquestionable authority. It had been worth waiting for.

Dran yawned. "When is we getting to Tammulcor?"

"Soon, Dran peDran. Be patient."

Easy to say, Kris thought. He scowled as the deests barrelled through a muddy marsh and kicked up a shower of brackish water. This trip would *never* end.

Somehow, he managed to hold himself in check for

the rest of the long day. Toward nightfall, the Great Light began to dim rapidly, and soon the nightly drizzle started coming down.

"Do we camp for the night?" Dran asked.

Without turning his head, Kris said, "No. Let's keep going."

They kept going. Before morning, the harbor of Tammulcor came into view. Smoky fires trailed upward, giving sign of violence the night before.

"There's been trouble here," Kris said. "And there'll be more." There was a note of keen anticipation in his voice.

The Great Cor Bridge across the Tammul River was guarded by a group of ten husky men wielding heavy truncheons. One of them was armed with a cocked and loaded rifle—an expensive weapon, but an effective one. The guard, Kris thought, looked as though he could handle the gun effectively enough.

They had placed a heavy wooden barrier across the bridge, just high enough to prevent even a trained deest from leaping over it. As Kris and Dran trotted their mounts up to the barrier, one of the men stepped forward to meet them.

Before the Peaceman could say anything, Kris called out: "Who are you? Why is the bridge blocked?"

"Peacemen!" said the burly one. "Who are you, and what is your business?"

"My compliments to the Uncle of Public Peace," Kris said smoothly. "I can see that he chooses his men well."

"What do you want? Why do you go to Dimay?" the Peaceman repeated, obviously attempting to ignore the naked flattery. But his voice was less harsh than it had been.

"I am Kris peKym Yorgen," Kris said. "Merely a citizen who wants to go to Tammulcor. Is that wrong?"

"Not wrong," said the Peaceman. "Merely foolish. The whole province is in an uproar; there is rioting in the cities and bands of looters in the country. You take your life in your hands to enter Dimay."

"Is that why you're here then?" Kris asked with feigned innocence. "To warn travellers?"

The Peaceman shook his head. "No. Somewhere in Dimay, someone has hidden eight million weights in cobalt. We don't want it to leave the Province."

"Indeed? Eight million weights?"

"Yes. You may enter if you wish, but watch yourself. And don't try to pass an exit barrier without stopping."

"Of course," Kris said meekly.

The barrier was lifted, and Kris and Dran urged their deests across the bridge.

"What is all that for, Captain?" Dran asked as soon as they were out of earshot.

"They're playing it smart. They didn't ask us if we had any coins when we came in, but you can bet your life we'll never leave with any. They're letting cobalt into the Province, but they're not letting any out."

"I wonder why," Dran said slyly.

"I wonder!"

They trotted on across the Great Cor Bridge.

The first task at hand was to find lodging and a place of business. Then, Kris thought pleasantly, once things were set up, things would really begin to pop in Tammulcor.

The city was quiet, just now, but it looked as if it were about to explode into violence any minute. An uneasy fog hung over the port, and even the usually placid Tammul River looked oddly threatening. Restless townsfolk moved aimlessly about the streets, and here and there an ugly-looking little knot of men was gathered, whispering earnestly.

"The first thing," Kris said, "is to find a place to stay. Suppose you get moving into town and find some hotel with room for us."

Dran nodded. "And then?"

"I want to find an office for us. We need a center of operations. I'll go look for that, and you meet me back here at midmeal. Got that?"

"I sees perfectly," Dran said.

"I hope you does," said Kris.

Kris rode down into the heart of town, watching carefully for sign of an office building that would serve his purposes. He needed one centrally-located, impressive-looking, and easily defended in case of emergency.

After about half an hour, he found what he wanted. He hitched up the deest and strode inside. A thin youth with blinking eyes looked up lazily at him from a chair in the vestibule of the building.

"Yes?"

"I'm looking for the landlord," Kris said. "I want to rent an office."

"He isn't here," the boy said.

"When will he be back?"

The boy shrugged complacently. Kris took a step closer to him and grabbed him by the scruff of his tunic.

"Hey, let go of me!"

"Not so much noise," Kris said mildly. "Where's the landlord, now?"

"He's—upstairs," the boy said.

"Get him," Kris commanded.

The boy dashed away, not bothering to conceal the fact that he was happy to be out of Kris' reach, and returned a few moments later with a sour-faced man of middle age. The landlord confronted Kris with an expression of unhidden hostility. Kris noticed that a wide-bladed peych-knife was thrust in the sash of the man's trousers.

"You the fellow who wants an office?"

Kris nodded. "My name is Kris peKym Yorgen. I'm interested in renting one of your vacant suites."

The landlord clamped his lips together and grimaced owlishly. "We don't have any vacant suites," he said.

"Oh? That's odd; I'd say the building was at least half empty, from the looks of things."

The man's hand slipped to the pommel of the peych-knife, but he made no move toward Kris. "I say the building's full, and I say I don't want any strangers renting here. What are you going to do now?"

Kris shrugged. "Well, if you're going to be that way about it—"

Casually, he drew a thick sheaf of purple-and-gold Bank of Pelvash scrip from his pocket, riffled through the notes reflectively, smiled, and stuffed the roll of bills back in the pocket. He drew forth a handful of cobalt coins, jingled them, and likewise replaced them. Then, whistling a sea tune, he turned and sauntered toward the front door.

"Just a minute," the landlord said hesitantly as Kris started to leave. "What kind of business you say you were in?"

"What does it matter?" Kris countered. "The building's all full, isn't it?"

The landlord smiled craftily. "That was Bank of Pelvash money you had there, wasn't it?"

"What of it?"

The landlord put his palms together. "Possibly I could find a vacancy," he said. "Quite possibly."

The sign on the door said: SCRIP EXCHANGE OFFICE. Kris grinned as he looked at the reversed printing on the inside of the frosted glass door. It looked impressive. If Dran were doing his duty, spreading the word around Tammulcor, it wouldn't be long before the good folk of the town would be clawing at each other to see who'd get inside that door first.

Gently, he slid open the desk drawer and looked down at the handgun that lay there. It was one of a pair, the other of which was concealed inside his belt, covered by his vest.

They were handsome weapons, lovingly made, a fine pair of the few handguns in existence. The rifle had become a fairly common weapon in recent years; some student at the Earthmen's school had invented it for use by the farmers in the days of the Great Depression, when, because of the superabundance of crops, the herbivorous forest animals had multiplied like wildfire. The farmers had needed something to hold them off when they became hungry in the second year.

They were expensive because they had to be made of specially treated iron; bronze would be much too weak to withstand the violence of the powder unless the weapon were reinforced—in which case it would be too heavy to carry easily. And there was, of course, no need for a weapon like that. What good is a gun so big you can't carry it?

The pistol was Norvis peKrin's idea. Instead of one charge, it carried four in a little revolving cylinder, each with its own cap. Norvis had been very careful about allowing *that* secret to leak out.

Thus far, very few people had realized the effectiveness of such weapons against men—although there were undoubtedly a few farmers in Dimay who were learning fast, and certainly the Peacemen had recognized it.

Since the rifle was designed to kill at long range, it

was necessarily long enough to give proper distance to the copper projectile. But Norvis' idea had been to make a short-range gun for personal protection. It didn't need to be as big or as heavy, because it carried less powder and had a shorter barrel.

Someone else might think of the idea—but unless he had Norvis peKrin's ingenuity, the gun would only fire one shot without reloading—not four. As he studied the gun, Kris reflected that perhaps he had been underestimating Norvis a little.

Suddenly he heard footsteps in the corridor. He pushed the desk drawer closed and looked up.

There was a shadow on the other side of the frosted glass, and then a timid knock.

"Come in," Kris said.

The short, stocky man who opened the door was obviously a farmer. His hands were calloused, and he wore the heavy cloth of a field worker. In his belt was a long peych-knife.

"Are you Kris peKym Yorgen?" he asked cautiously.

Kris flashed his most winning smile. "I am. What can I do for you?"

"Well—well—" The man took a deep breath. "I heard somebody say that you were redeeming Bank of Dimay notes. Is that so?" His tone was querulous, timid, as though he was certain he was about to be called a liar.

"Perfectly true, my dear fellow," Kris said. "A ten-weight Dimay note will bring you a five-weight note of Pelvash."

Without hesitation, the farmer pulled a wad of bills from his belt pouch. "These ain't no good at all. Nobody will take them. I got two hundred weights here, but I can't spend them."

Kris opened the drawer in his desk. On top of a huge pile of Pelvash notes lay the heavy pistol, which he pushed casually aside. He took out twenty five-weight notes and counted them ostentatiously.

"Here you are, sir. One hundred good Pelvash notes for your Dimay money. May I see them?"

He took the Dimay notes, leafed through them, and dropped them into another drawer. Then he handed the Pelvash bills to the farmer. "It's a pleasure to do business with you, sir."

"And you, sir," the farmer said. His eyes glittered; obviously he still did not quite believe such a windfall could occur. He mumbled his thanks, suspiciously counted the notes, and left hurriedly.

Kris watched him go, and chuckled in amusement. It was a good business, he reflected. If only it worked the right way!

At this very moment, Kris thought, Dran peDran is roaming around the town telling people of the fabulous fool who was buying up the worthless Dimay scrip at two-to-one. And now there was a farmer who would also spread the tale. Before long, how worthless would the Dimay currency be?

By mid-afternoon, there was a line forming that stretched out of Kris peKym's office, down the stairs, and out into the street. Business was booming. The word was getting around Tammulcor rapidly.

One at a time, Kris took care of each customer, ushering him into the office, giving them a winning smile and half their money back—in cobalt-backed notes of the Bank of Pelvash.

It was a long day. By the time the Great Light had begun to fade, he had collected nearly sixty thousand weights in Dimay bills, and had paid out half that in

Pelvash scrip. The drawer that held the redeemed Dimay currency was overflowing.

And then it happened—the thing that Kris had been half expecting all day. Two men stepped into the office. One of them, a swarthy one with a heavy scar drooping over one eye, walked up to Kris' desk and suddenly jerked a heavy peych-knife out of his belt. The two-foot blade, with its blunt end and razor-keen edge, was poised six inches from Kris' throat.

At the same time, the second man drew his knife and stationed himself at the door, facing the crowd outside.

"Nobody's going to get hurt if they behave themselves," he said roughly. There were several men in the crowd who were carrying the heavy knives, but none of them did anything except shrink back from the doorway.

The man with the scar held his knife steady. Kris stared evenly at the thin edge before him. He could be decapitated with one flick of the stranger's wrist, and it was not a pleasant thought.

"Give me your Pelvash notes!"

"Certainly, sir," Kris said. His voice was not loud, but it carried to the crowd outside. There were murmurs, but the people on line still did nothing. Tammulcor was used to this sort of violence by now.

"You may have the notes," Kris continued. "I don't care to lose my life." He reached toward the drawer. "It's obvious that you need the money, or you wouldn't take such desperate measures. Of course, it's a shame that all those people out there won't be able to get the money they deserve, but—"

There was a sudden low growl from the crowd outside. They had heard Kris' words. They knew what was going on.

The man holding the peych-knife at Kris' throat

turned his head just a fraction as he heard the sound from outside. That was all Kris needed. One hand hit the robber's wrist, sending the heavy knife ringing across the room. The other hand, balled into a hard fist, slammed against the man's ear.

The robber dropped soggily.

With a leap, Kris cleared the desk and landed on the back of the second man, who had heard the noise but hadn't dared turn his back on the crowd.

Kris wrenched the knife from his hand and slammed him up against the wall. The man shook his head groggily as Kris whirled him around and grasped him by both lapels of his vest.

"Now, what's the idea?" Kris' voice was oddly gentle.

Helpless in Kris' grasp, the would-be robber said, "We—we're longshoremen. We're out of money. No ships have loaded for a week!"

"Here! What's going on here?" bellowed a voice from the door.

Kris jerked the man he was holding, spinning him around. He grabbed an arm and twisted it sharply behind the man's back, at the same time turning to face the door.

Two Peacemen were pushing their way through the crowd. One customer armed with a peych-knife was standing over the other robber, who was just regaining his senses.

"Come in, Peacemen," Kris said, without releasing his hold on his adversary. Then, to the customer with the peych-knife: "Thank you, friend. You may step outside; the Peacemen are here now."

The man glared at the fallen robber and then walked back into the corridor with the crowd.

The Peacemen pushed the door shut. "We heard

there was a robbery here," said one Peaceman, keeping a firm grip on his thick black truncheon. "Looks like you've got it fairly well under control, though." He waggled his club at the scarfaced man on the floor. "Come with us, you; we're going to see the Uncle of Public Peace."

"Just a minute, Peaceman," said Kris mildly. "Could I have a word with you?"

"What is it?"

Kris lowered his voice. "These men are my bodyguards. We put on this little act for the people outside, just to show them that I could take care of myself."

"Oh? But why?"

Gradually Kris relaxed his pressure on the longshoreman's arm. He made no untoward move, so Kris released the arm completely.

"Well," Kris said, "I handle quite a lot of money here, and I was afraid there might be a robbery. I know that you Peacemen have enough to do already, and a good citizen should do all he can to help, so I thought that if word got around that I was able to handle my own affairs, I'd have less trouble." He patted the longshoreman on the back. "With the boys here to back me, we won't need to take Peacemen from their more important duties."

The Peacemen were smiling. "Why, that's a very good idea," said one. "Scare the tough boys off, eh? You're very thoughtful."

"I try to do my best," Kris said deprecatingly. "Don't I, boys?" He glanced at the two longshoremen.

"You sure do, sir."

"Yes, sir."

The words came out as a duet.

"Thanks for coming, though," Kris continued. "It's good to see such fine Peacemen."

"We were right outside, really. One of your customers called us in. What sort of business do you run here, anyway?"

Kris smiled and explained carefully. Within three minutes, the Peacemen were carrying Pelvash money, for which they had handed over their worthless Dimay cash.

"By the way," Kris said when the transaction was finished, "would you mind waiting outside for my boys? It would add color if the crowd thought they'd been arrested, and if they try to walk out by themselves they're likely to get killed."

"Certainly, sir. Glad to do the favor."

When they were outside, Kris faced the two longshoremen. They looked shamefaced, and, as Kris slowly looked them over, they grew nervous.

"What's your names?" he asked.

"Bor pePrannt Hebylla," said the scarred one. "He's my brother, Bryl pePrannt."

"You look like a couple of pretty tough boys," Kris said. He paused for a moment. "If you want a job with good pay, come back here tomorrow morning."

"You mean that?"

"If I didn't, you'd be on your way to the Uncle right now. All you have to do is let those Peacemen escort you out of here."

He handed each of them a five-weight Pelvash note. "Go out and get yourself cleaned up. Take a bath. If you're not here by the Hour of Second Prayer, don't bother."

They nodded and left without another word.

Kris turned. There still were customers waiting to be served. He kept going until it was well after dark. Then he went to the door and announced to the impatient crowd, "The office is closing now. May the Great Light illumine you."

One man stepped forward.

"I've just got—"

"Sorry," Kris said firmly. "That's all for today. Come back tomorrow, if you want to redeem your Dimay money."

"But—will the offer still hold?"

"Certainly," Kris said, loud enough for everyone to hear. "The offer's good indefinitely. So long as you've got Dimay scrip, I'll be offering half as much in Pelvash money for it!"

He packed the day's receipts carefully in a bulging leather case, went out the back way of the building, unhitched his deest, and rode swiftly toward the hotel in which he and Dran peDran had rented rooms.

Dran was waiting for him.

"How is it go, Captain? I doesn't understand what's going on, but I does my best today."

Kris chuckled at the Bronze Islander's simplicity. "Everything's perfect, Dran! Business is wonderful!" He tossed the heavy leather case on the bed. "Watch that." He pulled a handgun from his belt. "There's my pistol," he said. "Use it if necessary. Someone might have found out where we are and decided to take the loot. I doubt it, but there's not much use taking chances."

"Where's you going, Captain?"

Kris stripped off his vest and shorts and substituted a pair of common seaman's shorts, a uniform of somber black. He grinned secretively at Dran peDran. "You do your rumor-spreading by day, youngster, I'll do mine by night!"

He headed out into the Tammulcor street.

6

Half an hour later, Kris strolled into a tavern, looking like nothing more or less than an ordinary seaman. The tavern was full and the peych-beer flowing; it was a time of troubles, and business was good.

When he produced cobalt coin to pay for his drinks, the barkeep practically fawned on him.

"What's yours?" he asked, staring at the hard money glinting in Kris' hand.

"Peych-beer," Kris said. The bartender fetched a glass of the heavy, warm Dimay brew, and Kris dropped his coin on the bar. "Light illumine you," he said. "What's the news around here?"

"May He illumine us all," said the barkeep. "There's nothing much, seaman. Just the same as yesterday."

It was the standard reply of the Tammulcor barman, ritualized, uninformative. It was social custom, nothing more. The real news would be forthcoming.

The barkeep pushed out the mug of brew and said: "There's a rumor around town that some fool is buying up Dimay scrip."

Kris grinned inwardly. He had figured that that would be the news of the day, and he had been right. It was unusual enough an event to cause comment all over town—perhaps it had even spread farther.

"Oh?" he said languidly. "Buying up Dimay scrip, eh? It doesn't surprise me at all. I'll give you one for two right now."

The tavern owner looked a little startled. "You mean that?"

Kris nodded emphatically. "Sure!" He reached into his pocket and pulled out a fistful of crumpled Pelvash notes. "Here's twelve weights. Want to give me twenty-four?"

The tavern-keeper's eyes flickered greedily. "You've got a deal, seaman." He handed over a sheaf of Dimay notes, which Kris promptly pocketed.

"That's a good profit for me—when the cobalt comes back to the bank."

He walked out, whistling.

The same thing was repeated, with variations, all over Tammulcor. Kris arrived at his hotel room much later that evening, tired and somewhat overloaded with peych-beer, but with his pockets stuffed with Dimay scrip. Things were beginning to move, he told himself happily.

"Dran? Dran, you here?"

There was no sign of the Bronze Islander. Kris shrugged and turned to the bed, where he spied a note written on a grimy piece of paper. It took him a while to decipher Dran's near-illiterate scrawl, but finally he concluded that it was a message telling him that Dran peDran had gone out for some entertainment, and would be back later.

Kris nodded. He didn't mind a few moments of privacy at all. He walked to the closet, reached upward, and hauled out the saddlebags of his deest. Quickly, he unpacked one of the pockets.

The first item to come forth from the saddlebag was a thickly-folded wad of paper—Del peFenn's instructions on what Kris was to do in Tammulcor. Kris remembered the way Del's grizzled, fierce face had looked as he handed the instructions over.

"Here's what you're to do, lad. Scout around, try to turn popular sentiment to us and away from the Elders, and above all stay out of any fights. I've outlined some speeches you can make."

Kris leafed through the pages. They were filled with Del's usual hysterical anti-priesthood tirades, the same sort of stuff Del peFenn had been handing out for so long to people obviously unwilling to listen. Casually, he ripped the sheets lengthwise, then tore the halves a second time, and ripped what was left into tiny fragments that he sprinkled into the waste unit.

"Del peFenn," he said softly to himself, "I bid you farewell. From now on, Kris peKym Yorgen is doing this *his* way."

The next thing to come out of the bag was a much-tattered but carefully folded sheet of paper. It was a standard seaman's map of Nidor, but it bore markings that Kris himself had made.

As he looked at it, he could picture men moving—men as well-trained, as efficient as his own sailors: men trained to fight together as seamen worked together on a ship; men who could follow orders without question; men who combined the fighting efficiency of Peacemen with the coordination of a ship's crew.

And he saw their target: The Bel-rogas School of Divine Law.

The Earthmen had no weapons; nearly a hundred years of dealings with them testified to that. But—what of their supernatural powers?

Kris glanced at the spot on the map which indicated the Holy City of Gelusar. There was his answer.

If the Earthmen were demons, or simply impostors, then the Great Light Himself would aid those who fought them. Their supernatural powers would be of no avail.

If they were, on the other hand, the true Messengers of the Great Light, then Kris peKym Yorgen, self-convicted of blasphemous sin, would die.

There was no necessity for decision now; he had decided long ago. The Earthmen must go. So far as any Nidorian knew, none of them had ever died, but there was always a first time—and that time would come soon.

He would still need Del, of course. It was Del's money—his private fortune plus the money he had solicited and wrung from the merchants and seamen for fourteen years—that was being spent in this effort to bolster the economy of Dimay and bring it under control of the Merchants' Party.

Kris looked at the map again and smiled grimly.

No, he corrected. *Not under the control of the Merchants' Party.*

Under the control of Kris peKym Yorgen.

The Council of Elders had been led astray; it would take a man who could see clearly to bring them back to their senses.

Beyond the fighting men, he could see another scene—a hundred or perhaps a thousand years in the misty future. A time when Nidor was as it should be, as it had once been—quiet and serene, with each following the Law and the Way of the Ancestors.

And perhaps—perhaps—the name of Kris peKym Yorgen would rank high, near the name of his Ancestor, Bel-rogas Yorgen, the Lawyer. Perhaps it would be—Kris peKym, the Exorcist.

Kris shook his head as though to clear it. The peych-beer was giving him delusions of grandeur, he decided.

He sketched idly in the margin of his map, thinking. Norvis had told him strange things about the Earthmen—about their secret city in the depths of the Mountains of the Morning, the city which only a few Nidorians knew was there; about their unfathomable schemes, and devious craftiness.

Kris was not sure how true all these stories were. But the facts spoke for themselves. Since the coming of the Earthmen, Nidor had undergone change.

Ergo, the Earthmen had done something to Nidor.

Conclusion: drive the Earthmen off the planet.

It was a concept he had broached unsuccessfully to Del peFenn. Del, with a merchantman's dislike for the priesthood, had been far more interested in going after the Elders than in bothering with the remote and incomprehensible Earthmen.

Kris licked his lips reflectively and peered close to the map. *If we approach from the west,* he thought, *we can bypass Gelusar and still wipe out the School.*

Del would kill him if he knew Kris was planning any such maneuver on his own hook. But Del was safely up there in Vashcor. Kris had the situation completely to himself down in Tammulcor.

But I need an army, Kris thought. He stood up and glanced out the window at the struggling wanderers in the street below.

Tammulcor was full of bewildered, unhappy people looking desperately for someone they could put their faith in. *What better material for my army?* Kris thought, with savage glee.

During the next few weeks, Kris began to feel amost

as though he was a disembodied spirit. He was detached from reality, watching what was happening in Tammulcor without actually being a part of it. It was an odd feeling for a man who was accustomed to shape events around himself.

For one thing, the money-changing business dropped off sharply. People no longer seemed willing to make the two-for-one exchange.

Kris kept close touch with what was happening in the troubled city. Combining business with pleasure, he adopted his role as ordinary seaman and went the rounds of the taverns again, saying nothing, simply standing to one side and observing.

At one place, he watched a small-time merchant enter and order a brew. The merchant, a chubby, surprisingly cheerful little man, stood around a while, and then said to the bartender:

"Have you got any Dimay notes about? I suppose you've thrown most of them away, but if you want to get rid of them for cash, I'll—"

"Forget it," said the barkeep crisply. "Dimay money is just as good as any other, these days. I'll take *your* Dimay notes, if you have them."

A flicker of surprise passed over the merchant's face. "But they aren't backed by cobalt! They're worth nothing whatsoever!"

The tavern-keeper grinned toothily. "Oh, so? Then why are you willing to pay for them?"

There was a moment of silence. Then the merchant smiled and shrugged without self-consciousness. "You're on to it, then. Well, it was a good racket while it lasted. For nearly a week, I was getting two and a half weights Dimay for one weight Pelvash."

"Sure," the barkeep said. "And at the same time, this Kris peKym Yorgen was offering two for one. And he isn't getting any more offers these days either."

Kris finished his drink and strolled out into the street. He had heard all he wanted to hear. It had worked! By offering a false backing to the notes of Dimay, he had made them worth something again. And as long as he wanted to, he could control the situation.

The net was starting to tighten. Even at this moment, Dran peDran was busily spreading another rumor. The people of Tammulcor were learning that the reason that the Council had held up replacing the cobalt in the Bank of Dimay was because the Earthmen had ordered the Council to stay away from the whole affair.

Dimay money was hanging in abeyance—and, for the time being, it had recovered its old value.

Three weeks after his arrival in Tammulcor, Kris was sitting in his office—alone. No one had come in to have money exchanged in the past two days. Why should anyone, when Dimay money was again on a par with Pelvash? But Kris was expecting company at almost any moment. A third rumor had gone fluttering through the town.

He didn't have long to wait. A visitor arrived not much past midmeal.

"I am Venk peDor Ghevin," said the man who entered. He was short and heavy, with something oily about his appearance. "You are Kris peKym Yorgen?"

"Correct."

"I am in the jewel trade. I understand you are offering one Pelvash weight for each two Dimay notes. Is this true?"

"No longer," Kris said. "I've just received word that the Earthmen have ordered the Council not to back the Bank, as they were intending to. I'm sorry. Dimay money no longer has value."

The jeweler's face became bleak with disappointment. "I'm sorry too. I had hoped you wouldn't confirm the bad news that just reached me—but you have. I've lost a great deal on this trading of notes if nothing comes through."

Kris leaned back in his chair and eyed the little jeweler with what he hoped was an expression of deep sympathy. "It's a nasty situation. But save your notes, Venk peDor. When I speak to the Council again, I may be able to convince them that they should go against the Earthmen's wishes. If so—and I see no reason why I should fail—you may redeem your notes with me."

"I see," said the merchant, making an ineffectual attempt to conceal his astonishment. "Very well, then." He bowed politely and left.

Kris chuckled warmly when the jeweler departed. *A big lie,* he thought happily, *is always worth a dozen little ones. If it's implausible enough, they'll always swallow it.*

Four more merchants swallowed it before Kris was finished for the day. Again, word began to travel through the city. Gradually, people were getting the idea Kris wanted to impart—that he was a powerful man who could swing the currents of currency virtually at a whim.

By nightfall, he was ready. If everything had worked out right, Dran peDran should have started his riot by now.

7

The warehouse of Nibro peDom Lokness, owner of the
Tammulcor Baker's Merchandisery and leader of the
Baker's Guild, was an imposing building at the upriver
end of town. As Kris peKym rounded the corner that
led to the warehouse, he saw there already was a mob
of rioters on the scene. Flickering torches cast a red
gleam over the building's walls, and angry shouts arose.
 "Where's Nibro peDom? We want bread!"
 "We want bread!"
 "Bread!"
Kris slipped into the shadows and watched as the
rioters hurled stones and imprecations at the massive
warehouse. The sides of the building were beginning to
blacken with smoke. Tension was accumulating in the
hungry mob.
 He nodded to himself. Tension. That was the key: set
men in conflict, draw the net of tension around them,
tighten. They react blindly. They can be led. They can
be manipulated. Coolly, levelly, Kris peKym calculated
the dynamics of the mob before him, and wondered if
Nibro peDom would make his appearance before the
anger of the mob surged over and caused the destruction of the warehouse. He hoped so.

Nibro peDom did not disappoint him. He appeared suddenly at the door of the beleaguered warehouse, with three Peacemen standing at his side.

"What's the trouble here?" the bread merchant demanded, in an angry voice.

"Give us bread!" someone shouted.

"Bread?" Nibro peDom asked. "You want bread?" He shrugged. "Bread costs money to produce, my friends. Give me money, and I will give you bread."

"All we have is Dimay money!"

"Worthless," Nibro peDom replied. "Mere paper. Eat *that,* if you like."

"But you took Dimay money last week," roared a burly man in the front who had appointed himself spokesman.

"That was last week," the merchant said evenly. "Last week, the stranger Kris peKym Yorgen was redeeming Dimay money. This week he refuses. Dimay money is worthless!"

"If you won't give us bread, we'll take it!" yelled a high-pitched voice. "Let's break in!"

The crowd began to surge forward uncertainly. Kris waited until they had a reasonable chance to approach Nibro peDom, and then leaped out of hiding and stepped between the merchant and the mob.

They kept coming. The big man who had been spokesman barrelled into him, and Kris hurled him back against a mass of shadowy bodies. Someone's fist struck him heavily; he grunted and returned the blow. The Peacemen behind him waded into the mob as well. Kris ducked under them and jumped up on the steps of the warehouse, next to Nibro peDom.

"*Hold everything!*" he roared, in a voice that could be heard blocks away. "Stop fighting!"

"It's Kris peKym," someone's astonished voice said.

"Yes! It's Kris peKym!" He held up his hand for quiet, and gradually the threshing mob settled into an uneasy calm.

"What's the trouble here?" Kris asked, turning to the bread merchant.

"These people want bread," Nibro peDom said. "And they offer Dimay money for it."

"So? What's wrong with Dimay money?"

"Nothing backs it," Nibro peDom said.

Kris laughed and turned to face the mob again. "This breadman says he won't take your money. All right; there are other bread merchants. Go somewhere else. But tomorrow, when you come to my office—I'll redeem your Dimay money again!"

An audible gasp swept through the mob. Kris glanced at Nibro peDom again. The merchant suddenly looked terribly flustered and confused. He stepped close to Kris, and whispered a few words in his ear.

Kris turned to the mob once again. "All right—Nibro peDom says he'll sell you bread—*tonight!*"

A roar of enthusiastic approval went up from the crowd. Kris smiled in satisfaction and whispered to Nibro peDom, "You can exchange your money tomorrow at my place—if you want to."

As he had assumed, only a few people showed up the next day, and none of them were there to ask for money. They were merchants. Among them was the baker, Nibro peDom Lokness.

There were eight of them, ringing themselves in a little semicircle around Kris' desk. They tried to look grim, although their faces betrayed more puzzlement and consternation than anything else.

Nibro peDom stepped forward to act as spokesman. He maintained a stern expression as he spoke, but there was respect in his voice, and he used the proper form of address to a superior.

"Old One, we have come to ask what is being done about the state of the moneys of Dimay. We have asked our priests, and they tell us nothing. You seem to know, so we come to you."

"Sit down, my friends," Kris said smoothly. "Care for some beer?"

The businessmen arranged themselves uneasily in the chairs against the wall while Kris brought each of them a foaming mug of brew.

When they had each taken a thirst-whetting sip, Kris leaned forward, his elbows on his desk. "Can I trust you gentlemen?"

They glanced at each other, and then all eyes focussed on Nibro peDom. The baker said: "You can trust us."

Kris opened a drawer of his desk and took from it two books—the Scripture and the Law. They were bound together, as was customary, by a copper band.

"I must ask each of you to give his word, bound by a promise to the Great Light, that you will not reveal to anyone else what I tell you today."

Make it impressive, he thought. *The more impressive it is, the deeper it'll sink in.*

He laid out the book. After a moment's hesitation, Nibro the Baker took the double volume, held it to his forehead, swore. The others followed.

When they had finished, Kris said: "The truth is this. The Earthmen have brought destruction upon Nidor. It is they who control our destiny—and the Council of Elders is powerless. If we are to return to the Way of our Ancestors, we must thrust out the Earthmen."

Nibro peDom slapped his hand to his leg. "That's *exactly* what I've thought all along! I've—I've been afraid to voice it openly, but—"

One of the other merchants rose. "I'll wager the Council *wants* to replace the stolen money, but the Earthmen won't let them!"

Kris nodded. "Thus far, my influence with the Council has held off the desires of the devil Earthmen, but I can't hold off much longer without help."

"What sort of help do you want?" Nibro asked.

Kris gestured with his hands. "We have to go to the aid of the Council," he said. "The Council *needs* us. Under the influence of the Earthmen, they're helpless. They have been unable to appeal to us—the common people. We must back our priesthood and throw the Earthmen off Nidor!"

"You say the priesthood is controlled by the Earthmen?" asked a small merchant in the corner.

"Of course," Nibro peDom said scornfully. "It's obvious, isn't it?"

Kris nodded. "We either help the Council against the Earthmen or we will be destroyed."

"Do you have a plan?" the baker asked.

"Of course I do," said Kris. "But I want you to think the matter over before I tell you what's in my mind."

They turned to one another, and a hushed buzz of conversation rose. Kris knew what they were thinking.

Here, they thought, was a man who knew when money was good and when it was not. He was a strong man, a man who knew how to lead. He was a man who knew what was good for Nidor.

Nibro the Baker turned to him and said, "We're with you, Kris peKym. We'll follow where you lead."

He could barely keep from jumping with glee. He could see the towers of the Bel-rogas School bright with flame even now, and old Del peFenn blustering with impotent rage as his young disciple singlehandedly drove the Earthmen from the planet.

Kris glanced from one man's face to the next. They were angry, impassioned-looking men. They would follow his orders. He had them in his hand, now.

Here's the nucleus of my army, Kris thought. *We'll start organizing at once—and march on Bel-rogas!*

He rubbed his chin thoughtfully, wondering just where he should begin to outline his plan to his eight merchants. But just as he was about to speak, he heard a rapid, excited knocking at the door.

"Just a minute," he said, frowning. He crossed the room and threw open the door.

A tired, bedraggled-looking man stood there, his body hair gray with roaddust, swaying wearily, seeming as though he would collapse at any moment.

It took Kris a moment to recognize him. *"Norvis!* What's happened? What are you doing here?"

The Secretary coughed, "Step outside a moment, Kris."

His mind a frozen blank, Kris followed Norvis out into the hall, ignoring the puzzled glances from the merchants within. He grasped the smaller man by the shoulder and whirled him around to face him. "What's going on, Norvis? Why are you here?"

Norvis seemed to gasp for breath. "We need you. We need help, and you're the only one who can give it now."

"We? Who's *we?* What are you talking about?"

"Del peFenn's daughter and son—and I. We had to flee Vashcor; someone is after our lives!"

Kris blinked unbelievingly. "Your lives? What about Del?"

Norvis peKrin's face became bleak. "Del peFenn was murdered two days ago. Shot from ambush by a rifle. We don't know who did it."

8

Kris stared at the smaller man almost without seeing him, as the meaning of his words began to filter through his mind.

"Del is *dead?*"

Norvis nodded. "He was killed in the street, right outside the Headquarters. He was about to enter the building when someone shot him down. I saw the whole thing from my window."

"You know who did it?"

"Couldn't see," Norvis said, shrugging. "I have some ideas, but—" He paused. "Del was getting awfully fiery about overthrowing the Elders, and I knew it wouldn't be long before someone tried to silence him."

"Nasty situation," Kris said, almost to himself. He glanced back into the room where his eight merchants were sitting waiting for him. "Look—I've got eight fine, dues-paying members of the Party in there. They don't know that they've been in the presence of their new Leader all morning."

Norvis frowned, then nodded. "You *are* the new Leader, of course, now that Del's dead. You sure you can do it? It's a big job, Kris—and getting bigger."

"Don't worry about that. I'll be able to handle it."
He rubbed his chin thoughtfully with the back of his
hand. "It seems to me, though, that you should have sent a
messenger instead of coming yourself. Who's handling the
Party in Vashcor? You didn't leave young Ganz in charge,
did you?

"No. Ganz and Marja came with me; I figured that if
anyone were out after Del, they might try for his children,
too. I left the Party in Captain Bas peNodra's hands. He's
a nobody, but he can hold them together if there's stronger
leadership from the top. I thought maybe you'd rather
keep up the work here than go back to Vashcor."

"You were right," Kris said decisively. "There's more
work to be done here in Tammulcor in a week than there
is in Vashcor in a year. I think we'll set up our new headquarters here—make this the center of the Merchants' Party.

"But there's time for that later. Here's some money.
You take Ganz and Marja down to my hotel. Dran
peDran's there; he'll take care of you. We'll talk this
out when there's some free time. Right now, I've got
business to attend to."

Kris turned and went back into his office. The conversation the eight merchants had been engaged in died away
immediately. They looked up at him, and he surveyed
them with icy eyes—eyes that showed neither friendliness
nor hatred, only an expectancy of obedience.

He glanced at each of them in turn. "You are all members of the Merchants' Party, aren't you?"

The men looked at each other briefly, and then, as
though he were afraid something would happen to him,
the baker said softly: "Yes. We are."

Kris peKym's expression didn't change. "Then give your
alms to the honor of Del peFenn Vyless, who has been
murdered by our enemies."

"*What?*" Nibro peDom was out of his chair instantly. "How do you know that?"

"The man at the door just now was Norvis peKrin Dmorno," Kris said. "He bore the news from Vashcor."

"What will happen to the Party now?" Nibro asked nervously. "Now that Del is gone, who—"

"From now on, you will follow me," Kris said coldly.

"You? But who are you?"

"Kris peKym Yorgen, and that's all that need concern you. Del chose me his successor before his death."

"But how do *we* know that?" the baker asked truculently.

Kris frowned. "Because I tell you so! Do you think I'd *lie?*"

Nibro peDom seemed to give ground. "But—what are your qualifications? You're not a merchant. What do you know of our special problems? As far as *we* know, you're just a travelling moneychanger!"

Kris stepped forward and placed a forefinger on the baker's chest. "Nibro peDom, be assured that I know the merchants' problems intimately. I also know the problems of the seamen, the bankers, the farmers, and the priests. I have their interests at heart—as well as those of the Great Light. The Party is in good hands, Nibro peDom." He folded his arms. "And now, let's get down to business, shall we? I called you here for a reason, and we've already wasted too much time."

The meeting took nearly an hour. By the time it was over, Kris had obtained several definite commitments. Mentally, he checked off the things he would have to remember—there were things to be delivered and things to be set aside and stored.

"Let's run through it again. Drang peBroz, two thousand peych-knives."

The merchant nodded. "Nearly three feet long, heavier and wider in blade than normal, with a special thong to loop around the wrist. A very odd peych-knife, Kris peKym."

"That's not for you to worry over," Kris said.

Quickly, he reviewed the contributions each merchant was to make. "All right," he said finally. "Is everything understood?"

"All but one point," said Kresh peBor Dmorno, a pale-skinned wine-merchant. "What of the money?"

Kris looked at him steadily for a moment, then said: "If you can't give your share, why are you here?"

Nibro peDom, the Baker, glared Kresh peBor down. "We will give, Kris peKym," he said.

"Good. Don't worry about going broke; there'll be money to spare. You may not make an immediate profit, but the reward will be greater when the Earthmen are gone. Got that?"

They nodded. Kris smiled satisfiedly; he was beginning to make things fall in line. The meeting was closed with handshaking all around. The merchants filed out, while Kris remained, jotting down a few notes on what had taken place.

A good day's work, he thought. *We're moving in the right direction at last.*

He locked the door of his office, pocketed the key gaily, and trotted down the stairs, in a hurry now to return to the hotel.

It was late at night, Kris saw, when he emerged into the street. The falling night-rain splattered on the pavement and dribbled from the darkened roofs of the buildings into the street below.

And for the twentieth time in as many days, Kris heard footsteps behind him.

Every damn night! he thought. *Why?*

It had been going on far too long, and it was irritating to Kris to have a more-or-less constant shadow. So far, nothing had been attempted. Kris had managed to catch a glimpse of the man now and then, but whoever it was had never been close enough to be a danger. To make sure that no trap was being set, Kris had taken a different route home each night. He hadn't been attacked yet—but he didn't like the idea of being followed.

It would have been a waste of time to attempt to elude the pursuer; the man, whoever he was, obviously knew where Kris lived and where he worked. To waste his energy every night trying to get away from the shadowy figure would be just that—a waste of energy. So Kris had simply kept his eyes and ears ready, waiting for whatever might happen.

This night, the footsteps sounded closer than they had been. Kris kept his ears cocked. The city was dark; the wind had whipped up and blown out many of the street lamps.

He passed a darkened alleyway, and, quite suddenly, three men came charging out toward him. They said nothing, and it was obvious that they intended to kill to get the money Kris was carrying.

Kris went for his gun. He jerked it out of his belt and levelled it at the first of the oncoming attackers. There was a horrendous roar and a great belch of smoke and flame. The man paused, startled, but Kris could see that he hadn't been hit.

He came on again, as Kris thumbed back the hammer for a second shot. There was another blast, and this time the first man dropped, almost at Kris peKym's feet. The other two were still coming; Kris had to make both of his next shots count. Otherwise—

Suddenly, a third figure appeared out of the wet gloom, coming up behind the attackers, a huge peych-knife swinging in his hand. The blade slammed home twice, and the two remaining thugs were lying dead in the street.

Kris kept his pistol levelled at the newcomer.

"Don't shoot that thing, Ancient One!" said a half-frightened, hoarse voice. "It's me, Bor pePrannt Hebylla!"

It was the scarfaced man who had attempted to hold him up when he had first come to Tammulcor. He stepped nearer, his peych-knife lowered. "Did they hurt you, Ancient One?"

"No," said Kris. "You came along just in time."

"I did my best, Ancient One."

Kris shoved his pistol back into his belt. There were noises up and down the street, now; people were peeping cautiously out of their windows, wondering what the two bursts of noise had meant.

Kris jerked his head in the direction of his hotel. "Come along; no use waiting for the Peacemen."

Bor pePrannt shoved his knife into his belt and fell into step.

"Why didn't you and your brother come back to my office that day?" Kris asked.

"Well—to tell the truth, Ancient One, we didn't know what to expect. We argued about it, my brother and I, until it was well after the Hour of Second Prayer. When we realized it was too late—well, it was too late."

"My brother got aboard a ship, so he gave me the money you gave him. He went to Gycor—there's work there."

"And you?"

"Oh—well, I've been getting on. Odd jobs here and there in the daytime."

Like a handful of pyramid dice, everything suddenly fell into place. Kris stopped and looked at his rescuer. "Hoy! Is it *you* who's been following me around at night?"

"Why, sure, Ancient One. I wouldn't want you to get hurt just because my brother and I argued that morning."

"Great Light!" Kris said, trying to keep from grinning. "Come along, Bor pePrannt. You have a job—permanently."

They arrived at the hotel without further incident. Kris and Bor pePrannt climbed the stairway and strode down the hall to the suite which Dran and Kris occupied. Kris reached for the handle of the door and started to pull when the door swung open unexpectedly. Kris stepped back and blinked.

Marja geDel was standing there, looking almost shamefully beautiful in view of what had happened to her father. Her deep, wide eyes held a sparkle, and beneath her vest, her body seemed incredibly alive and exciting. Her long legs seemed to shine in the lamplight that poured from the room.

"Kris!" Her smile was radiant. "It's good you're here; we've been discussing everything, but we couldn't arrive at any decisions without you." Then her eyes narrowed a little as she saw the hulking figure of Bor in the dimness behind Kris. "Who's that, Kris?"

Kris stepped into the room, with Bor following him. "Bor—step out and introduce yourself."

The scarfaced man smiled hesitantly and said: "I am Bor pePrannt Hebylla, Old Ones."

Briefly and concisely, Kris explained to Marja, Ganz, Norvis, and Dran what had happened and how he had come to meet the broad-shouldered longshoreman.

Dran peDran who had been sitting on a chair against the far wall, stood up with a wide smile and walked over to grasp Bor's hand. "We is needing good men with a peych-knife. How is you learn to handle one? You doesn't look like a farmer."

Bor grinned lopsidedly. "I'm not. I've been a seaman, but I couldn't keep from getting seasick; I tried being a Peaceman once; but I was let out because I didn't attend prayers at the right time. So I took up longshoring."

Kris looked at the two men. Here was his nucleus, he told himself. Here were the prototypes of the kind of men he wanted.

He turned to Norvis, who was sitting cross-legged on the bed. "Now let's get straight what happened in Vashcor. Exactly what happened to Del?"

Norvis didn't get a chance to answer. Young Ganz, standing near the bed, said: "Some foul son-of-a-deest shot him while he was going into his office! Someone in the hire of the priesthood!"

Kris looked at the boy. "I didn't ask you, youngster. I asked Secretary Norvis."

Ganz subsided, and Norvis said: "It happened just about as Ganz said. Del was walking toward the office. Someone fired a rifle at him; the copper slug went right through his head."

Kris rubbed his knuckles over his jawline. "It sounds as though the priests might have been partly responsible. I doubt that an ordained Grandfather would have done or even condoned any such thing, but considering Del's attitude, some young hotheaded acolyte might have done it. After all, Del wasn't exactly friendly toward them; the Party lost a lot of backers because of his policies. They weren't too well calculated to win the approval of the people."

Ganz peDel bristled instantly. "If you mean he went after the dirty priesthood too hard, you're wrong. It isn't possible to go after those old mothbags too hard. And when I catch up with the Elder who shot Del . . ."

"Oh?" Kris interrupted. "Was it an Elder who assassinated your father?"

"Well," the young man said defensively, "that's what everyone's saying. And I don't see why not. It's logical, isn't it?"

"Of course," Kris agreed. "But logic doesn't always hold together in times like these. Words lose their meaning; friends become enemies. Policies change."

Norvis, who had, as yet, said nothing, finally asked: "Are there going to be changes in our policy now?"

"Damned right there are!" Kris turned on the Secretary fiercely. "Look, Norvis, I've felt for a long time that we were going about things the wrong way. Well, here's my opportunity to do things the *right* way. Our first step is to win back the people Del alienated—the farmers, the majority of the masses of Gelusar, even the priests themselves."

"The priests?" asked Ganz peDel. "What do you want *them* for?"

Kris folded his arms. "Because the priests help to hold this world together. Because they *belong* on Nidor. Because they follow the Great Light."

"Is we going to have to work with the Elder Grandfathers?" Dran asked. "I doesn't believe I trusts them."

"It isn't a matter of trust," said Kris. "It's necessity." He leaned forward. "What Del and the rest of you forgot is who the real enemies are—the enemies I plan to channel my attack against."

"You mean the Earthmen?" Marja asked.

"Of course the Earthmen! *They're* the devils who've been causing our troubles—and they're the ones whom we must fight! Not the Elders, I tell you."

He glanced around, saw general agreement on their faces. "Any questions?"

No one spoke. "Good. That's official policy of our Party from now on. Norvis, you can take that down."

"Does you has anything definite in mind?" Dran asked.

Kris smiled slowly as he prepared to deliver the words he had nursed in his mind so long. "Yes," he said. "Yes, I know what the first objective is."

He stared at the five faces before him. "We must destroy the School," he said slowly. "We must wipe out Bel-rogas completely, so that not even a memory remains!"

"You'll need backing for that," Norvis said.

"I'll get it," Kris told him flatly. "By the time I'm through, I'll have every man on Nidor behind me."

"What about the women?" Norvis asked.

"What about them?" Kris didn't quite see what the Secretary was driving at. "Women can't fight; they have nothing to do with it."

"I know they can't," agreed Norvis. "Women can't fight. So what do they do when faced with an emergency they can't handle physically? They pray, Kris—they *pray*. And a wife has a great deal to say about what her husband does, whether you realize it or not. Is a woman going to allow her husband to fight the very thing she pins all her hopes, her strength, her very *life* on?"

Kris chewed at his lip for a moment, then nodded.

"You're right. That's probably part of the reason Del didn't succeed. He attacked the priests—the same priests who were such solace to the wives and daughters of the very men Del wanted to win over." His eyes narrowed. "That means we'll have to change the women's views, too. But how?"

"I think I know," Marja said suddenly.

"Go on," Kris said.

"Well, look. As you said, the women depend on their faith in the Great Light to support them when their physical strength can't help them. If we can show them that the Earthmen have alienated the Great Light, we'll have them on our side. After all, the Earthmen have only been around for six Cycles of years—the Great Light has been watching over us for untold thousands of Cycles."

Kris glanced at Norvis. "What do you think?"

"I agree," Norvis said emphatically. "If we can convince the people that the Earthmen are devils from the Outer Darkness, and at the same time convince them that we are really on the side of the priests and the Great Light, we'll have them in the palms of our hands."

Kris turned back to Marja. "Very well, then. Your job will be to convince the women. I think it's a job that only a woman could do. Have you any ideas on how to go about it?"

"Yes," Marja said proudly. "I'll go into the temples and the marketplaces and just talk. Gossip—no more. I'll tell them about the Party and Kris peKym; I'll suggest that the Earthmen—not the priests—have caused all our trouble. I'll put it to them that the priests need our help—the help of the Party—to drive the demons out. I'll start bad rumors spreading against them."

"What about the School?" Norvis interrupted.

"That too," Marja said emphatically. "Have you noticed how many promising students have been expelled from the Bel-rogas School of Divine Law lately?"

Norvis grinned wryly. "Yes. So?"

"Very well. Those students have mothers and sisters. Do you know why they were expelled? I'll tell you: They were *too* smart! The Earthmen knew that they were just about to discover that Earthmen were demons—or at least they were on the right track. So they were unjustly expelled."

The others all smiled.

"Great!" Kris said. "Great! That's the right attack!" Then he paused and looked at her carefully. "But you'd better do something about yourself. You don't look like a common farm woman."

"Oh, I'm not," Marja said, suddenly looking very demure. "My father is a priest—a Grandfather in Sugon. I'm in Tammulcor visiting relatives."

Norvis burst into laughter. "Girl, you're perfect! Absolutely perfect."

Kris chuckled in agreement. "Right. All of her father's virtues and none of his faults."

Ganz peDel broke in then. "Is there anything *I* can do?" His voice sounded eager and—perhaps—just a trifle hurt.

Kris looked thoughtful. "Well, I—"

"He can help me," said Norvis quickly. "The Secretariat has a great deal of important work to do, and Ganz will be very useful."

"Good enough," said Kris. "Meanwhile, Dran and I will be training men. I have an idea for a group of men who would be a sort of Peacemen group of my own. Those who qualify will be well paid."

Bor pePrannt said: "I can teach them to use knives, Ancient One."

"Good," said Kris.

Later, when the others had gone to bed, Norvis raised the first objections.

"I can't see it. Just scraping up an army and marching into Bel-rogas like that—it can't go. I don't like it, Kris."

"Why? Great Light, why?" Kris gestured angrily. "Look here, Norvis—all my life, I've hated those devils, and I know you hate them too!"

Norvis' face darkened. "And for good reason," he said bitterly.

"All right, you hate them," Kris persisted. "And now that I propose to smash them down, you draw back. Great Light, Norvis, what's going on in your head?"

Norvis sat back and gently smoothed his ruffled down. He was silent for a moment. When he spoke, he seemed to be choosing his words with utmost care.

"Kris—you're not a plotter. You're a fine leader, but you can't see more than three days into the future. I agree that the Earthmen should be wiped out—the devils—or at least driven back to the sky they came from."

"So?"

"Not your way, though. Not by just busting in there and wrecking the place."

Kris frowned quizzically. This had happened time and time again in the past, and he was getting not to like it. He would present a plan, carefully thought out and closely reasoned, and Norvis would hew it to threads in a moment's time.

Who is this Norvis anyway? Kris asked himself. *He thinks he's smart, and I'll bet he thinks he can run me. Well, he never has, and he won't start now.*

"We'll attack Bel-rogas next week," Kris said firmly. "My way. I've got the approach strategy all worked out."

"All right," Norvis said wearily. "But you'd better start wearing a brass hat if you don't want to rejoin your ancestors as fast as Del did."

"What do you mean by that?"

"I mean that you won't outlive the gutting of Belrogas by a month," Norvis said quietly.

"Are you dictating policy to me?" Kris demanded.

"Far from it," said the Secretary. "Just offering my opinion."

"Your opinion's not needed," Kris snapped. "I'll manage by myself."

"Very well." Norvis closed his eyes for a moment. Then, changing the subject, he said, "Oh, by the way— what do you plan to do with all that cobalt we have cached away on the Bronze Islands?"

"What does that have to do with—"

Suddenly Kris paused, stood up, smiled slyly as a thought occurred to him. *I'll show Norvis who's a plotter,* he thought vehemently. "Go get Dran peDran. Wake him up."

"What for?"

"We're journeying to the Bronze Islands tonight."

Norvis' face wrinkled. "You're—why?"

"You'll see," Kris said. He didn't elaborate, and he made sure that the expression on his face would discourage Norvis from asking any further questions.

9

The *Krand* left the harbor of Tammulcor a week later, carrying Kris, Dran, a crew of eighteen picked men, and a noisy, restless cargo of deests. The false bottom was also in use. Eight million weights in cobalt lay hidden there. It had been a quick bur arduous job, getting the cache out of the Bronze Islands earlier in the week.

They pulled out of the Bay of Tammulcor and headed north up the river Tammul. A dinghy-load of Peacemen cut across their path before they had gotten very far upriver, and a tall man at the front of the small boat held up one hand.

"Hoy! Who are you, and where are you heading?"

"Captain Kris peKym Yorgen," Kris replied. "Heading for Gelusar to market these deests." He gestured at the herd on the deck.

The Peacemen looked up at him suspiciously for a moment. Kris waited impatiently. They were still worried about their missing cobalt, evidently—but since the recent upswing in Bank of Dimay currency, they were somewhat relaxed. Kris hoped he wouldn't be put to the nuisance of another three-hour search; a delay of that length might be utterly damaging to his project.

Finally the Peaceman said, "Deests, eh? Very well, head upriver. They'll probably stop you again at the Bridge of Klid, though."

"Thanks," Kris said. "I appreciate the clearance. Any news of the missing cobalt, by the way?"

The Peaceman shook his head. "All is quiet. We're sure we'll find the money soon, though. No one's being allowed out of Dimay without full search."

"Wise move," Kris said. "I hope you won't search fruitlessly for long."

"Something tells me the cobalt will come to light soon," the Peaceman said. "Good voyage to you, Captain."

"And a pleasant night to you," said Kris. "Great Light illumine you."

"And you," the Peaceman replied.

The dinghy glided away. "All right," Kris yelled. "Up river to Gelusar, now!"

It was early evening as they passed under the Great Cor Bridge, out of the environs of Tammulcor, and up the sluggish Tammul. The Great Light had begun to set, the Lesser Light was not yet in evidence, and the air was moist with promise of the evening's rain yet to come.

Kris stood on the deck, listening to the quiet complaining of the deests. Behind him, Tammulcor shrank in the distance; Gelusar lay far ahead upriver. The night was still young. If they made good time, they would reach the landing point just about this time the following night.

After a while, Dran came out on deck.

"Everything is well, Captain."

"Good," Kris said. "It's going to be a tough trip, sailing upriver."

From the starboard came the cry of one of the men, calling out the sounding.

"All well," Kris yelled back. He peered out at the wide, flat stretch of water ahead. The Tammul was a shallow, sleepy river, and Kris had little mind to run aground in the night—not with eight million weights of cobalt on board.

"Here comes the rain," he murmured to Dran, as the nightly drizzle began to sprinkle down. "Better get the deests under."

"I is just about to do that, Captain," Dran said. "Hoy there! Drosh! Marn! Down with those deests!"

Kris stood alone on deck for a while, then strolled aft to the helmsman.

"Not much wind tonight, is there?"

"No, Captain," the helmsman said. "It's a hard night for sailing, Captain. A very hard night."

Kris nodded and walked away. It was a very hard night indeed.

Morning came, and the *Krand* was still a good distance from its destination. Other boats were moving downriver from Gelusar, heading toward Tammulcor, and occasionally a wandering Peace dinghy would cut by, peering suspiciously at the ship without hailing it. It was the river patrol, on guard for strange craft.

By the time evening had arrived, the journey was nearly over. Kris peered ahead into the gathering dusk at the shore to the westward, searching for the landing.

"All right," he said after some time. "There's where we go ashore." The *Krand* moved silently through the dark waters to the inlet, and they dropped anchor as close to shore as possible. Kris called the men on deck.

"We're landing here," he said.

"I thought we were going to Gelusar," a deckhand said. "Isn't that where we're going?"

"We're going to Bel-rogas," said Kris. "And it'll be a lot easier to leave the river now and finish the trip overland than to try to carry eight million weights of cobalt through the heart of town."

Dran nodded. "Is right. We is about ten miles from Bel-rogas now. Is not so bad."

"We'll have to make three trips, Bronze Islander," said Bor pePrannt unhappily. "We've got a hundred manweights aboard, and twenty deests. The best of our animals can't do better than two or three manweights of cobalt."

"Not so," Kris said. "Each deest's going to carry *five* manweights."

"We can't do that!" Bor pePrannt protested. "They can't carry that much!"

"They can if we walk alongside of them instead of riding on their backs," Kris said. "We've only got ten hours till dawn. If the Great Light rises while we're still in Bel-rogas, we're finished. We'll have to make it in one trip and no doubt about it."

He looked around. "Everyone understand, then? Dran, get your crew down and start unslinging the cobalt from the hold. Bor, get a couple of men and drive the deests out on shore. We can't waste any time."

It was a strange sight—twenty deests, each groaning and swaying under a fortune in cobalt, each with a man walking at its side urging it along.

The Lesser Light glimmered faintly above as the caravan wound its way through the narrow dirt paths that led to Bel-rogas. Kris and his crew had anchored ship about two miles below the Bridge of Klid that spanned the Tammul, and, under cover of nightfall, they were heading west and north toward the School.

Two roads forked out from the Bridge of Klid—one going directly into Gelusar, the other bypassing the Holy City and carrying outward to Bel-rogas, which lay some five miles west of Gelusar. Kris guided his caravan through the backroads and byways to the fork, and then along the little-travelled road from there to Bel-rogas.

The coins jingled faintly as the deests struggled along under them. It was not, thought Kris, exactly a quiet group travelling along the road. He fingered the butt of the pistol at his sash; in case anyone should come down the road from the School, there might be trouble. It wouldn't be easy to explain where they were heading in the middle of the night with eight million weights of cobalt.

There were no difficulties, though, and finally they reached the borders of the School. Spacious parks bordered Bel-rogas; standing on the outskirts, Kris could see the group of majestic, Earthman-designed buildings located around the central campus, and the spreading lawns that surrounded the entire School. All was quiet.

It had taken five hours to cover the ten miles from the Tammul to the School. Five hours yet remained before the Great Light rose. Five hours to plant the cobalt and get moving back to the *Krand*. It was more than enough time.

He paused for a moment, mopping away the rain that had soaked into his eyes, and listened to the noisy breathing of the deests. They were struggling under the heavy load of coins, and some of them were scraping at the ground with their hooves. They couldn't bear the burden too much longer.

"Let's go this way," Kris said. "Get the deests in line and follow single-file."

Stealthily, he edged into the grove that led to the

School. He brought the caravan to a halt about half a mile from the nearest of the buildings. No one was around, though a light burned in a window of the building.

"Unload the deests," Kris ordered. "And don't clank those loops of coins around too much."

He joined them in the job of unloading, and before long eight million weights of cobalt lay in a deceptively small pile on the grass. Kris turned to Dran. "Pick two men and start driving the deests back to the ship. I don't want them bothering us while we work."

"We could always drive them down into the School and stable them there," Dran suggested.

"It wouldn't do," Kris said, chuckling. "The idea lacks practicality."

Dran chose his men and began herding the deests back out of the School grounds. Kris turned to the others.

"Unload those shovels," he ordered. He picked out four men and said, "You come with me. The rest of you deploy yourselves in a loose circle around us."

Each of his four chosen men grabbed a shovel and Kris led them as close to the School building as he dared. "We dig here," he said.

The eight million weights of cobalt took up more than thirty-six cubic feet. That meant a pit three by three by four, at least. Shovels bit into the ground.

It was slow work, because Kris insisted on a tidy job. When one of his men showed signs of tiring, he sent him back to be replaced with a fresh digger. They had the pit finished within three hours; the first glimmers of the Great Light were beginning to filter through.

"In with the cobalt, now," Kris said. He watched as they lowered the heavy loops of coin into the ground and painstakingly replaced the turf over the pit. They scattered the displaced dirt at the bases of several trees. Kris stepped back to survey the job.

"You'd hardly know anything was under that hump in the ground," he said approvingly. Then he chuckled. "Let's get back to the ship. The Earthmen are going to have a hard time explaining *this* away!"

10

The next few months moved slowly, as far as Kris was concerned. They were months of waiting, of exasperating detail-work and fine-lined planning. Slowly, he began to organize the sort of group that he felt would best serve his needs.

It took delicate juggling. Norvis peKrin took over the Scrip Exchange Office, carefully keeping the sagging monetary system of Dimay on a fairly even keel. But the paper scrip of Pelvash was nonetheless running dangerously low. Fewer and fewer people came in to exchange their money, true; since they assumed that it must be worth something, they were reluctant now to give it away for half its price. The money had acquired an artificial backing which consisted solely of Kris' pledge to redeem it for Pelvash money—a pledge that no longer mattered. It hadn't taken long for the Merchants' Party to accumulate several million in Dimay scrip by their trading policy. It now was back at its earlier value—and Kris and Norvis had thereby doubled their capital.

Meanwhile, Kris started his training program. It involved much word-of-mouth activity, a technique he was rapidly becoming proficient at, and before long he had assembled a fairly large corps of young men, drawing them from the landless farmers in the outlying districts, from the irreverent sailors willing to jump their papers, from anyone else who wanted to serve. Under the leadership of Dran peDran and Bor pePrannt, the men drilled every day in the flatlands just north of the city. No specific target had been revealed, but the men enjoyed the discipline.

Young Ganz peDel began to show promise, too. Norvis had suggested that he, too, be trained, and at first Kris had been reluctant. But the boy showed he was made of the right stuff. He could handle a peych-knife as well if not better than the others.

He had worked up a rather clever little exercise for the men. They formed up in a column on their deests, and then, galloping full tilt at a wooden pole, each man swung at it with his knife, lopping a bit off the top. Of course, as it grew shorter, each man had to bend lower to get his bit off. It improved their aim with the knife tremendously.

Yes, Ganz showed promise.

Marja geDel was doing her job well, too—even brilliantly. Kris became definitely aware of it the day a loutish-looking farmer in his thirties came to the office and asked to join Kris' men.

"Why do you want to join?" Kris asked.

The lout twisted his fingers together. "Well, Ancient One, I understand I can make a little extra money, which, Light knows, we need. My wife said she'd manage the farm; she said it was time I did something to help drive the devil Earthmen away. I never thought much about it, but she's right, I guess. All the women seem to think we've got to do something."

"We do," said Kris, hiding a grin. "Report to Garf peDom's farm tomorrow—just outside of Tammulcor, on the Tammul Road. That's our training field. Come at the Hour of Second Prayer."

When he had gone, Kris thought over what he'd said. The women were definitely coming round. Preparations, then, were nearing completion. Now other wheels had to be set in motion—and for that, he would have to resort to his skill at rumor-mongering.

"Is there anything to the story that the Earthmen robbed that Bank?" Kris inquired casually, one evening, in a Tammulcor bar.

The barkeep looked surprised. "Haven't heard that story myself. Where'd you pick it up?"

Kris shrugged. "Oh—it's all around. I thought you could give *me* some further information, that's all."

The barkeep leaned forward, interested. "Tell me about this, will you?"

"Seems the Earthmen—this is the way I got it—used some kind of magic to get into the Bank, and floated the cobalt out."

"No!"

"That's the story," Kris said. "They floated it right up to Gelusar, out to that School of theirs, and they've got it hoarded away some place."

"The devils!"

Another man came up—a seaman named Bort peDril Sesom, a man Kris knew vaguely. "What's this I hear?"

Kris told him.

"The Earthmen, eh? Well, I never did trust them, never did at all."

Meanwhile, far at the other end of the city, Dran peDran curled his wiry fingers around a mug of peych-beer and smiled confidently at the fat merchant sitting opposite him.

"It's the Earthmen, all right," the Bronze Islander said in a hoarse voice. "They is stolen the cobalt and buried it somewhere. I hear that everywhere."

"The Earthmen, you say? Stole the cobalt? Why'd they do that?"

Dran peDran shrugged eloquently. "Does you understand the Earthmen?" he asked.

"All I know about the Earthmen," the Merchant said, "is that I don't like them and I don't like their School. And if they robbed the bank—"

While in a third section of the port, Bor pePrannt Hebylla growled loudly. "It's the Earthmen! The devil Earthmen who have our money!"

People crowded close around in the bar. "What? The Earthmen? Where'd you hear that?"

"It's all over," Bor pePrannt said. "Everyone knows they took the cobalt!"

A long-nosed farmer with fiery eyes crashed his hand down on the table. "We ought to kill them!" he roared.

Someone else picked it up. "Kill them! Kill them!"

By the next morning, there was hardly a man in Tammulcor who did not suspect that it truly was the Earthmen who had robbed the Bank of Dimay.

Sentiment began to gather. Forces started to be exerted. The rumor spread—from Dimay to Pelvash, from Pelvash to Thyvash, around the coast from Gycor to Lidacor to the distant province of Sugon.

The Earthmen had robbed the bank!

It was on everyone's tongue—or rather, *almost* everyone. Two significant groups were yet to commit themselves to an opinion. No word was forthcoming from the Council of Elders—and no denial had yet emanated from the Earthmen at the Bel-rogas School of Divine Law.

"We've got them where we want them now," Kris said. "We have to keep our fingers on the pulse of the world. When the time is ripe—we strike against Bel-rogas."

"And how will you know when the time is ripe?" Norvis asked.

"Don't worry. I'll know."

Suddenly Ganz peDel appeared at the door of the room. Kris looked up. "What is it, Ganz."

"Visitors," the boy said. "Old men. I think they're priests." His face made no attempt to hide his distaste for the clergy.

The visitors entered, walking stiffly. They wore the blue tunics of priests, and over them light travelling wraps.

"Good evening, Ancient Ones," Kris said with respect.

"May the Great Light illumine you," said the older of the two priests.

"Peace of your ancestors be with you," Kris returned. "May I ask what brings you here, Grandfather Bor peDel?"

The Priest-Mayor of Tammulcor took a seat. "I think it is time I called upon you, my son." He gestured toward the man who accompanied him. "This is Marn peFulda Brajjyd," he said. "Priest-Mayor of Vashcor."

"Great Light's blessings," Kris said.

Marn peFulda nodded curtly. "You're Kris peKym Yorgen, are you not?"

"I am. And this is Norvis peKrin Dmorno, my assistant."

"We've already met," Marn peFulda said.

"Yes," said Norvis. "We know one another."

Kris frowned over that for a moment, then brushed it from his mind. "May I ask your business with us?"

"Briefly, this," said the Priest-Mayor of Tammulcor. "My colleague and I represent troubled areas of a troubled world. We fear for Nidor. We have long thought that Nidor has been in serious danger, and have given thoughtful consideration to that which must be done to—ah—hold things together."

"As have I," Kris said. "But—"

"We've concluded that something's got to be done about Bel-rogas," Marn peFulda said bluntly. "We won't mince words. You two have built up a powerful organization. We're here to offer you our spiritual and political support."

Kris stood up and crossed his arms in a by-now customary gesture of power. "I see. You're here to tell me that you're not in full agreement with the policies of the Council of Elders, I take it."

Marn peFulda spread his hands and smiled with delicate subtlety. "In a word—yes."

Kris frowned and glanced from one priest to the other. *Very nice,* he thought. *It's shaping up. It's taking form. Now I've landed two priests, and big ones.*

"You see," the Grandfather went on, "something must be done or our religion will be splintered. Already there is a man wandering around the countryside of Lebron, calling himself the New Lawyer; he thinks he is a second Bel-rogas. Something must be done to strengthen the Council and purify it of the influence of the Great Darkness."

"We understand you've organized some men," Bor peDel said hesitantly. "We would like to suggest—ah—"

"That you take them to Gelusar," Marn peFulda completed.

"Indeed?" Kris glanced at Norvis. "For what reason, may I ask?"

"There's a current rumor that the Earthmen were behind the robbery of the Bank of Dimay," Marn peFulda said. "You're aware of this, of course."

"Ah—yes."

"Very well. We have learned through ecclesiastical channels that Elder Grandfather Kiv peGanz Brajjyd has reluctantly decided to hold a public hearing—in order to squelch this rumor. The Earthman Smith has agreed to appear and speak in his defense."

"And you think," Kris said, "that the presence of myself and my men at this hearing might—"

"Might be worthwhile—especially if Smith's defense should appear particularly unconvincing."

Kris nodded. "I thank you for your information, Ancient Ones. I'll consider it carefully."

"May the Great Light illumine your mind as He does the world," Marn peFulda intoned.

"May He illumine yours," Kris responded.

After the priests were gone, Kris turned to Norvis, who had remained silent throughout the entire interview.

"Well? What did you think of that?"

Norvis smiled. "Encouraging, all right. How do you plan to deal with it?"

"I'll go to that hearing, of course—with a hundred of my best men."

"And the local situation, here in Tammulcor? Who'll be in charge while you're gone?"

Kris thought a moment. "Oh, pick one of the youngsters in the Party. Give him a chance to learn how to administer, while I'm away. Might as well not let the new blood go stale, you know."

"Good idea. How about Dran peDran?"

Kris shook his head. "Don't like. Dran's a clown. Besides, the men won't listen to a Bronze Islander."

Norvis snapped his fingers. "Say, what about young Ganz peDel? He could probably handle some of the job while you're in Gelusar."

Kris frowned. Ganz? Could be, he thought. "I suppose so," he said. "If you think he's worth the trouble of bringing along. But I guess they'll listen to Del's son, young as he is. All right—make Ganz peDel my deputy. I'm going to leave for Gelusar immediately."

11

The Tammul Road followed the Tammul River, winding its way from Tammulcor to Holy Gelusar on the Dimay side of the stream. It was wide and well-turfed, neither so hard that it hurt a deest's cloven hoof, as some of the desert roads did, nor so soft that the animal had trouble moving at a rapid pace. It had been built for heavy traffic, but it had never seen the traffic it had on a spring day in the Year of Brajjyd, in the 247 Cycle.

A hundred men, wearing the black vest and trousers of seamen, modified by splashes of bright scarlet across the back and the chest, rode in precision array on a hundred sleek deests. At their head rode Kris peKym Yorgen, and to his left, Dran peDran Gormek.

In a column four wide by twenty-five long, they trotted up the broad highway toward the Holy City. The thundering sound of the hooves of a hundred deests echoed in the air as they went on.

Word had already preceded them that Kris peKym of the Clan Yorgen was going to Gelusar to watch the Council of Elders question the Earthman, Smith; farmers lined the road, anxious to get a glimpse of the man who had saved their money from disaster, cheering the men as they rode northward.

"Bring back our cobalt, Kris peKym!" they shouted. "Get our money for us, Ancient One!"

Proudly, the hundred men followed their Captain, who seemed to ignore the accolades, but secretly was revelling in them.

He gripped his reins tightly with one hand and waved to the people. A few yards behind the hundred men came five more deests, and upon them rode men wearing the honored blue robes of the priesthood, two of them bearing the white slashes of Priest-Mayors. As they cantered by, the farmers bowed low, and their cheering ceased.

It was a good move, thought Kris, having the priests ride in procession with them. The very fact that the Council of Elders had seen fit to question the Earthman in public, and the fact that five priests were accompanying Kris peKym to the hearing, would deepen the suspicions of the Earthmen which had begun to take root in the mind of the people.

When the column rode into Gelusar, Kris noticed with pride that none of the men seemed to show the long hours of travel; they held their heads high and rode erect, like the well-trained soldiers they were. He knew no one would be surprised that the men were armed; it was foolish not to be armed in these troubled times, and a peych-knife was, after all, a handy weapon. The fact that these blades were half again as long as an ordinary knife went unnoticed.

Kris had already sent a man ahead of the column, riding at a hard gallop most of the way, to arrange things. By the time the hundred men reined up before the Inn of the Purple Deest, less than half a mile from the Great Temple itself, the arrangements had been made.

The innkeeper, a rotund, oddly gloomy-looking

man, came out in front of the old inn and held up a hand in greeting.

"Hoy, Kris peKym!"

"Hoy," Kris said. "We have travelled far, innkeeper."

They exchanged blessings, and then the staff of the inn showed the men to their rooms, while their deests were towelled and fed.

That evening, in the banquet hall, Kris was to address his followers. They were not the only ones present; there were townspeople there who had come to the Inn of the Purple Deest for their evening meal, curious to see the strong young man who had upset Nidor so greatly. Kris' words were meant for their ears as well as those of his own men.

The meal had been blessed by the Priest-Mayor of Vashcor, and when it was over, Kris pulled aside his plates and climbed to the top of the table itself. A sudden hush fell over the great banquet hall.

Kris let his eyes wander over the upturned faces for a moment. They were *his* men he saw—his own. They were tough and strong and eager, ready to follow the orders of their Captain.

"Youngsters," he said, "We have come to Holy Gelusar to right a great wrong. It has been said that the Priesthood of the Great Light has done us wrong—has betrayed us to the powers of the Great Darkness. Let us, in all honesty, admit that there is some truth in these charges.

"But let us not forget the greater truth. Let us not forget that if our priests have erred, they have erred as men, not as priests.

"We have with us, as you know, five priests, two of whom hold the noble position of Mayor. I have spoken to them concerning what has happened on Nidor in the past six Cycles—the past hundred years—and they agree on one vital point. The Earthmen are not, as they claimed, Messengers of the Great Light; they are Agents of the Outer Darkness!

"Our priests have been misled, true—but no more than we. And they, like ourselves, have come to see the truth. Why else would they question the devil Earthman in public? Our priests know what they are doing now; they see the Earthmen as they really are. As fiends! *As devils who have come to lead us from the Way of our Ancestors!*"

He paused, then continued in a softer voice, "Of course, not all of the priesthood sees the truth. Naturally, being men, some of them are still in error. But we should not hold this against the Priesthood as a whole. We should not hold our Ancient Grandfathers accountable as a group for the errors of a few.

"We have come here to witness the questioning of a devil, the Earthman Smith. We don't know what his answer will be—but we do know one thing. No demon, when spoken to in the name of the Great Light, can lie. We will know, then, Smith's true status. If he is a demon, he will be unable to lie. He will be unable to deny that he and his fellows have stolen and hidden our money. If he is but a man, he will be able to lie—but then we will have little to fear from him. In either case, our path is clear. Nidor and the people of Dimay must get their money back!"

Applause rang through the hall loudly, making it impossible for Kris to continue. Although he held up his hand for silence, it was some minutes before he got it. He noticed that the townspeople in the back of the banquet hall were cheering too.

When quiet finally came, Kris went on.

"It has been said that we—the Merchant's Party—are against the Priesthood and the Council of Elders. You and I know that this is untrue. It is true that our former leader, Del peFenn Vyless, who was murdered by some unknown enemy of ours, spoke against the Council. But he spoke against them because they were misguided, not because the Priesthood itself is wrong."

It was an out-and-out lie, and Kris knew it. But propaganda is propaganda.

"We have then, a job to do. But we must never lose sight of the fact that we are here to save our priests, not to condemn them. We are here because we want to see Nidor return to the Way and the Light! *And we will!*"

There was another prolonged burst of applause. Again, Kris signalled for silence.

"I will now ask Grandfather Marn peFulda Brajjyd, Priest-Mayor of Vashcor, to lead us in a prayer that those of the Priesthood who have not yet seen the truth will be given the truth by His All-Effulgent Majesty, and that the people of Nidor will again be blessed by His radiance."

The priest rose as Kris stepped down from the table. Looking grave and impressive in his blue robes, Grandfather Marn peFulda began the prayer.

The Square of Holy Light was jammed with Nidorians on the day that the hearing began. The huge open space in front of the Great Temple was overflowing with milling people, talking, whispering, shouting, and fighting. Here and there, little knots of people gathered to argue, quarrel, and trade blows.

Kris peKym Yorgen and his hundred men marched into the Square less than two minutes before the scheduled time of the hearing. In spite of the close-packed tightness of the mob already present, the measured tramp of their high-heeled riding boots automatically cleared the way for them. They marched directly to the wall of the Great Temple and stood quietly, waiting for the Elder Grandfathers to appear on the broad balcony above. The air was warm and clear; it was a good day for a public hearing.

At precisely the hour of Thanksgiving, an acolyte stepped into the tower of the Great Temple and swung a heavy mallet with ponderous dignity. The huge bronze gong that hung there sounded its mellow note across the city, and the crowd in the Square of Holy Light became silent.

Then the shutters of the balcony drew slowly aside, revealing the assembled Council of Elders in full ceremonial array. The bronze chains of their high office were draped across their blue and white robes, and their bronze coronets shone brightly in the glow of the Great Light from the eternally clouded sky.

At the left of the balcony stood the Earthman, Smith. He was simply clad, wearing a pearl gray shirt and trousers. The long sleeves and trouser legs made the clothing unlike any normally seen on Nidor.

But it was not his clothing that drew Kris' attention. It was Smith's physical appearance. This was the first time Kris peKym had ever seen an Earthman. The sight startled him.

In spite of the fact that the Earthmen had been on Nidor for nearly a hundred years, they were not often seen by the public. They kept themselves secluded at the School—and, while most Nidorians were aware of the presence of the alien men on their planet, few had seen them, except for the students at the Bel-rogas School of Divine Law.

Kris studied the Earthman carefully. He seemed

unusually big, as he stood there on the balcony near the Grandfathers. Kris had always thought of himself as an exceptionally big man, but it seemed to him that Smith was even taller than he was.

People said that the Earthmen actually did have body hair, but, if they did, none was visible to Kris. Smith's hands and face looked naked and pink, while his chin and the top of his head had, if anything, too much hair.

His topknot was dark except for the graying at the temples, and his beard was long and straight and thick. It covered his chin completely. The whole effect was oddly grotesque, but somehow impressive. It gave an appearance of great power to the craggy features.

Kris stood silently, his arms folded, waiting for the hearing to begin. He felt uneasy in the Earthman's presence, sensing someone even stronger than himself.

Another sound of the giant gong echoed across Gelusar. Kris' ears shook at the impact of the sound wave.

It rang a third time, and then Elder Grandfather Kiv peGanz Brajjyd, Leader of the Council, stood up. He held out his arms and crossed them in blessing.

"The peace of your Ancestors be with you always!"

"And may the Great Light illumine your mind as He does the world," Kris found himself mumbling in response.

Kiv stepped forward. "My children," the Elder Grandfather said, "We are gathered here together in the Temple of the Great Light to deal with a difficult and trying matter. The Elder Kovnish will conduct the inquiry."

At Kiv's gesture, a tall, ascetic-looking Grandfather arose and took Kiv's place.

"As the Elder Brajjyd has made clear, the matter at hand is a delicate one, and we are hesitant to expose our guides from Earth to the indignity of a public trial. Yet the Council of Elders—after due deliberation—has settled upon this method of clearing the reputations of the Earthmen and of the Bel-rogas School, whose name we all revere. I call upon the Elder Yorgen to sum up the reasons for this inquiry."

The Elder Kovnish stepped down and another Grandfather arose. Kris felt a little twinge of half-suppressed pride at the impressive sight of the head of his own clan. The Elder Yorgen was the second oldest member of the Council, second only to Ancient Kiv, and his down was silvery-gray in color.

"My children, not long ago a strange and frightening thing happened in the Province of Dimay. Unknown persons entered the Bank, and took from it eight million weights in cobalt." The Elder Yorgen paused for a moment, as if the energy required to deliver a speech of two sentences had sapped his feeble strength. "Where this money is, we do not know.

"However—rumor has become widespread that our friends of Bel-rogas, the Earthmen themselves, have taken this money. You all have heard these rumors. It is the opinion of the Council that such words border on blasphemy, inasmuch as the Earthmen have long been recognized as emissaries of the Great Light Himself. We are gathered here today to hear the public denial of the rumors from the lips of the great Earthman, Smith."

Kris' eyes flashed across the balcony to where Smith stood, impassive and aloof—Smith, the archdemon who had guided the School for more than forty years.

"Thank you, Elder Yorgen," said the Grandfather Kovnish. "The case has been stated. I call upon all of you present to witness the words of the Earthman Smith, here on this sacred ground."

Kris smiled. The Elders were playing right into his hands! Smith would be called on next—and, naturally, he would deny the charge, here in the Temple. What an uproar there would be, Kris thought, when the money turned up on the Bel-rogas grounds after all!

The Elder Kovnish gestured at Smith. "Earthman, we call upon you in the name of the Great Light to speak."

The Earthman rose.

12

He stood there, staring mildly at the assembled Elders. It was possible to count to ten before he spoke. Finally, he said, "Just what is it you want me to tell you?" His voice was deep, well-modulated, commanding, and there was something strangely alien about his accent.

The Elder Kovnish recoiled as if he had been struck. "What we ask of you," he said slowly, "is that you deny the charge now current among the people of Nidor that the Earthmen were responsible for the robbing of the Bank of Dimay."

Smith seemed to frown. "I'm afraid I can't do that," he said. "Is there anything else you want?"

What the devil is this? Kris thought bewilderedly. *Why doesn't Smith just deny it and get this farce over with?*

The Elder Kovnish said, "Perhaps you misunderstand, Ancient One—though I hesitate to imply that. The belief is that you of Earth caused the robbery of the Bank of Dimay. I ask you to tell us this is not so."

"How can I do that?" Smith asked.

A ripple of astonishment ran through the crowd this time. What was happening was utterly unbelievable.

"Am I to understand," the Elder Kovnish said sharply, "that you therefore *admit* the truth of the rumor that the Earthmen robbed the Bank?"

"I didn't say that," replied Smith.

"You neither admit nor deny guilt?"

Smith shrugged. "As you please. I hardly think the Bel-rogas School should be held accountable for its actions in so public an inquiry."

Exasperation was evident on the Elder's face. The hearing, Kris thought, had taken a bizarre twist. The Council of Elders appeared to be in great distress.

"How are we to interpret your answer?" the Elder cried.

"As you please," Smith said again. "You may draw what conclusions you wish. The Great Light guide you, Grandfathers—and now I must leave you."

Grandfather Kiv stood up, his face dark with anger. "Hold, Smith! You have left us in doubt—and it is not fair. We have asked you for a simple answer."

"And I have given one," Smith said boredly. "I'll repeat it, though: it is, simply, that I don't care to discuss Bel-rogas matters in public. Nor," he added, "will I answer your questions privately, Elder Brajjyd. I must go now."

And Smith nodded, stepped around Kiv, and quitted the balcony, leaving the Elder Grandfathers standing in a confused semicircle, their mouths opening and closing slowly in utter consternation.

Kris didn't understand what had happened, but he saw his chance and took it.

He turned to Dran and Bor pePrannt, who were standing next to him.

"Quick! Give me a boost!" He gestured at the carved, detailed figures on the wall ten feet from the pavement.

Both of them got the idea quickly enough. Within seconds, Kris had been lifted above the crowd. He reached out, tightened his fingers around an intricately-carved and fanciful gargoyle, and drew himself up, working upward onto the balcony.

The Elders were arguing among themselves when he pulled himself over the balcony rail.

"My name is Kris peKym Yorgen!" he bellowed.

The Elders looked at him in astonishment. "What are you—"

"I'm here to see justice done!" Kris roared. "You heard what that Earthman said, didn't you? Speak up. Elder Grandfathers! Did you hear him?"

The Elder Kovnish started to speak, but Kris cut him off in mid-syllable. "You heard him, all right! You heard him refuse to deny that he and his crew took the money! And why did he refuse to deny it? It's because they *did* take it! Can any of you claim the Earthmen did *not* steal the cobalt, now that you've heard the admission of guilt from the Earthman's own lips?"

Kris glanced around belligerently. The crowd below was completely silent, watching in awe. In the center, he saw his ring of a hundred loyal men.

The Elder Grandfathers were also watching him with something like awe. This was Kris' big moment; he was determined to play it for all it was worth.

"*I* say the Earthmen stole the cobalt, and I say I know where it is! It's buried on the land of that School of theirs! Come with me, and I'll dig it up for you!"

"How do you know this?" Grandfather Kiv asked stonily.

"I have my sources of information," Kris retorted. "Just as you Elders do. And I *know* the money's in Bel-rogas."

He looked down, saw the crowd beginning to move

impatiently, heard them talking among themselves.

A sudden blue-white glow attracted Kris' attention, and he turned his head upward to see what it was.

It was Smith—standing on the wall of the Great Temple. A blue-white aura of radiance surrounded him, and he was lifting himself into the air.

"Look!" Kris cried. "There's the devil Smith now—on his way back to Bel-rogas to hide the cobalt!" His pointing finger jabbed the air in the direction of the rapidly-dwindling figure of the Earthman, who was outlined for a moment in sharp relief against the grayness of the sky and then vanished in the general direction of the School.

"There goes Smith!" Kris shouted. "Back to Bel-rogas. Who's for going to the School to see what's there?"

"Just a minute," Grandfather Kiv protested feebly. Kris brushed the old man aside and lifted his hand toward the west.

"Your money's there, and I can prove it! Who'll go with me? Saddle your deests, and on to Bel-rogas!"

"Wonderful, is wonderful," Dran peDran exulted, as Kris made his way down from the balcony and into the threshing mob in the courtyard. "You is a marvelous speaker."

"Get the men together and get those deests up from the Inn," Kris ordered brusquely. "The mob's with us. It's our chance, now. Smith's talk left them all confused."

"To Bel-rogas!" someone cried. Kris glanced around. It was a stranger who had said it, a Gelusar townsman. Kris grinned. The fever was catching now. Soon, a mighty torrent of men would be behind him.

"Come on," Kris said. "Let's get out of here before

the Grandfathers realize what's up." He shoved his way through the mass of people and out into the street, with his men following behind.

"Get down to the Inn and get your deests," he ordered. "Then get back here."

Turning to the Gelusar people, he shouted, "Saddle your deests and ride with us! To Bel-rogas!"

Minutes later, Kris was astride his deest, a handsome, powerful creature whose long muscles throbbed beneath Kris' weight. Kris stood high in his saddle and swung his arm aloft.

Then he kicked his heel into the deest's side and began to race down the streets of the Holy City, past the Central Railway Terminal, through the crowded, heavily-populated West End of the city, and on out onto the Bel-rogas road. The thunder of a thousand deest-hooves clattered behind him as he rode.

Bel-rogas was five miles from the city of Gelusar, in a secluded area of foothills. The twisting, brown dirt road that led there soon became a river of dust as Kris and his men raced over it. Dust floated eye-high as they charged onward.

They were on their way at last, Kris thought excitedly, as he urged his deest onward. The Bel-rogas School was, at last, under attack. He glanced backward and saw a flood of men pouring after him.

Within minutes, the buildings of Bel-rogas became apparent.

Dran peDran drew up alongside him. "Where is we going first, Captain?"

"We'll ride right through the School and on to where we've planted the money. Once we've dug it up, the rest will follow automatically."

Dran peDran's round head bobbed as his deest lurched and raced ahead. The Bronze Islander's eyes gleamed. "I know what you means, Captain."

"There's the School!" Kris yelled. "We're riding right through!"

They climbed the gently-sloping hill and rode up to the massive but open and unguarded gate of the School. Kris laughed savagely and spurred his deest on. It plunged through the gate into the Bel-rogas School of Divine Law. "Follow me!"

They were in the midst of a vast green swath of well-kept grass which led up to a square, thick-hewn building surrounded by smaller ones.

Kris saw figures running toward him over the lawn, waving their arms at him and shouting angrily.

"You can't come in here! Go away!"

Students, he thought derisively. There were perhaps a dozen of them, with more in the background. He bore down on them, scattering them every which way as his deest burst into their midst, and continued on, through the main square of the School and out into the green field behind the central group of buildings. His keen eyes searched for the slight hump in the ground that would be the hiding-place of the cobalt.

For a moment he was unable to find it, and his body went cold with apprehension. What if the Earthmen had discovered the cobalt—had carried it away? What would he say to the people when it proved impossible to find the treasure?

Kris' fears were groundless. "There it is," he cried, pointing to a rise in the ground. He swung himself down from his deest almost in mid-canter, and Dran dropped lightly at his side.

"Get shovels! Start digging!"

They fell to with a will, while Kris watched impatiently. After some minutes of energetic digging, the first cobalt coin glinted from the ground.

Kris looked around and saw a tremendous crowd swarming over every corner of the field.

"Lift me up," he murmured to Dran, and the Bronze Islander and another crewman boosted Kris to his shoulders.

"Now give me a loop of coins."

They handed him a quarter-manweight loop of cobalt, and he swung it aloft. "See! See! The cobalt is here! The Earthmen have had it all along!"

"Kill the devils!" a powerful voice cried.

"Aye," Kris echoed. "Kill them!"

He held the cobalt high overhead, showing it to all in sight. The flame started to spread through the mob; he sensed their fury building toward a tremendous explosion.

"All right, put me down."

He dropped to his feet and hauled another loop of cobalt from the opened pit. Then he glanced at Dran. "Get all this stuff out of the ground, and have twenty men guard it. I'm going to see what happens down below at the School."

But the moment he sprang to the saddle of his deest he saw that there was no need to worry about the events at the School itself. The mob had already surged toward the buildings in the distance, screaming and shouting. Their raucous cries were thick in the air.

He urged his mount through the moving crowd of hysterical people, heading into the foremost ranks of the mob. Behind him came his men, a tightly-packed wedge.

A group of students had lined themselves up in a desperate attempt to forestall the angry townspeople. Young men and young women, holding clubs and peych-knives, stood shoulder to shoulder in defense of the School. Behind them stood a tradition of a century of scholarship—a fine tradition, but one that lacked the strength of the older one now resurging, Kris thought.

He didn't particularly like what happened, but there was nothing he could do. The armed mob halted only for a moment when they reached the defenders. Savage cries went up from the attackers, as, pushed forward by those behind, they found themselves in close combat with the defense line of students.

Knives and clubs swung bloodily, blades flashed in the air, men fell. The students didn't stand a chance. In less than a minute, they were overwhelmed and thrown back by the maddened townspeople.

The mob rushed on, stepping on and over the bodies of the dead and dying.

Thus far, there was no sign of the Earthmen or of the priests who taught at the school. Kris tried to keep his deest moving toward the school buildings, but the stupid animal kept shying from the crowd which surged around it like an angry sea.

The priests appeared then, holding their palms out before them in prayer. At least thirty of the blue-robed Grandfathers were there, clustered in a tight little group, offering their prayers and supplications to the Great Light and the Ancestors of Nidor.

But nothing could stop the mob. Those in front, who could see the priests, were pressed on by those in the rear who couldn't. The blue-robed men went down.

"A fire! A fire!" someone shouted. "Bring a torch!"

Kris scowled. There were valuable books in that School, papers and research documents that had been brought forth by five generations of students. Kris didn't want to lose them.

He started to cut off the man with the torch, then saw there was no point in it. The School had already been put to the flame. Fire was already bursting from the lower windows of one of the buildings. One—and then another and another.

The job was being done too well, Kris thought.

Where were the Earthmen? Had they left before the mob had arrived? Had they deserted their school in a sudden attack of cowardice?

Kris reined in his deest and held up his hand to signal his men to stop. The crowd was so dense that there was little to be gained by trying to push through it.

"Get back!" he called.

Like dry peych-beans in a heavy wind, the buildings caught. The flames wavered over the school, flickering and gathering strength. Building after building was put to the torch, until the entire campus was a raging hell of orange-red tongues.

"Look!" someone cried. "The Earthmen!"

"Where?" Kris demanded. He whirled in a full circle, ready to defend himself. But the Earthmen had no intention of fighting. They were gathered on the top of the Administration Building, which was already crackling with flames in its ground floor. Twelve Earthmen stood on the roof of the doomed structure, silently watching the crowd below.

Kris squinted. He thought he recognized Smith, but it was difficult to tell one Earthman from another in the blurring red light of the holocaust.

A rifle crackled. Then another spoke out. The Earthmen seemed to take no notice. A bright aura of blue-white light sprang up around them. Each Earthman seemed to stand in the center of a glow of light.

"The devils!" Kris murmured. As the hellish blaze from below licked up around them, the Earthmen ascended. One by one, they lifted into the cloud-laden sky, enclosed in their haloes of blue-white light. They rose upward, ascending higher and higher, drifting off into the sky, fading away from sight.

Kris watched as the twelve figures became tiny dots in the sky. At last, they were gone, seeming to fade into the clouds, and there was nothing left but the raging fire of the Bel-rogas School as the buildings collapsed into themselves one by one.

The Earthmen were gone.

Kris sat unmoving in his saddle, staring at the fading bluish sparks in the sky. He felt a sense of emptiness suddenly. They were really, actually gone—the dreamed-of goal had been achieved. Somehow, the idea that the Earthmen had been driven off Nidor was too incredible for him to grasp.

Then the emptiness faded as the realization came to him in full finality. *He* had driven them off. *He*—Kris peKym Yorgen.

He realized suddenly how still it was around him. He stood up in his stirrups and looked at the mob.

The mob had become something else—it was no longer a frenzied mass of destructive impulses, but simply a great crowd of individuals, all gazing silently at the sky. The only sound was the roar of the flames as they consumed what was left of the Bel-rogas School of Divine Law.

13

Kris and his hundred men rode into Holy Gelusar at the head of an oddly silent crowd of people.

He knew what the emotion affecting them all was, because he shared it. He was not ashamed of what he had done—merely awed at the magnitude of it.

Behind the column of mounted men marched four hundred more, each bearing on his back a great loop of cobalt coins weighing a quarter of a manweight. Eight million weights in cobalt—and yet almost no one thought about the money itself.

They marched into town. Those who had stayed behind lined the streets and began to cheer at the sight of the money. It was a vindication—a crushing proof of the iniquity of the Earthmen. Besides, it meant Dimay money was good once again.

Kris saw that the cheering seemed to brace those who had taken part in the sack of Bel-rogas. They seemed to stand a little straighter and walk a little more briskly, and the curious air of depression lifted.

By the time the procession reached the Square of Holy Light, the city of Gelusar was thoroughly aroused. A wild, demonstrative crowd preceded them, cheering and howling their joy.

"The story will be spreading," Bor pePrannt whispered to Kris. "It must be sweeping all over the city by now."

Kris nodded. "I know how it'll be. It'll keep getting more and more distorted every time it's told, until by the time it reaches the East End they'll be saying I throttled Smith with my bare hands."

He led his men into the Square and ringed them around it. Three streets led into the Square that faced the Great Temple, and Kris saw to it that each of the three was blocked with a deployment of armed and mounted men.

"Don't let anyone in!" he shouted. Then he stood up in his saddle and raised his voice so that all those who were already gathered in the square could hear.

"Leave the Square! Clear us room! Out! Move out!"

The shout was taken up, and, slowly, the people began to filter out of the Square and into the streets. Only the four hundred men who were carrying the coins were permitted to stay. They stood in the middle of the Square, hefting their loops of coins, looking proud of themselves and of Kris peKym. Rightfully so, Kris thought.

He wheeled his deest around and looked at the balcony of the Great Temple. It was shuttered and silent. Turning his mount again, he faced the men who carried the coins.

"All right," he said. "Let's put it where it belongs! Put it in a pile! Heap it up in the middle of the Square of Holy Light. Let's show the people what the devil Earthmen have done—and what they can do no longer!"

They began to drop their loops on a circular slab of obsidian that marked the center of the Square of Holy Light.

Loop after loop of coins jingled into the heap as the men threw them from their shoulders. Several of the copper wires broke, and the coins scattered, jingling and rolling over the pavement, while those outside the ring of mounted men watched in awe as the pile grew.

"Keep your hands off those coins!" Kris shouted. "The man who tries to take so much as a single weight will die!"

He signalled to the mounted men who blocked the streets, and the oversized peych-knives came out of their sheaths and were held high, their polished steel gleaming in the afternoon light.

It was an unnecessary precaution. The pile of coins was not touched. No one would dare, not with all eyes upon the Square.

And still there was no sign from the Great Temple.

Kris caught sight of Dran peDran and signalled him to come over beneath the balcony. Dran trotted his deest over to his leader.

"Does you want something, Captain?"

Kris pointed at the tower of the Great Temple, where the huge gong hung. "You're a good topman, Dran. Think you can climb up there and hit that gong?"

Dran looked startled for a moment, then grinned. "I does it, Captain." He turned his deest and headed for the wall.

Kris watched as the agile little seaman stood up on the back of his deest and leaped toward the same carved figures that Kris had climbed a few hours before. But Dran didn't stop at the balcony; he clambered on upward to the roof and then worked his way up the steeple to the great gong.

He reached his goal and waved cheerfully to Kris. Kris returned the gesture, and the little Bronze Islander picked up the heavy mallet that stood near the giant metal disk.

The reverberating note rang out deeply across

Gelusar, and the crowd became hushed. It was as though, Kris reflected, the gong itself had some tremendous power of its own over the people of Nidor.

"Again!" called Kris, and again the sound rang out, echoing in the still, humid air.

If it had an effect on the people of Nidor, it also had an effect on the Priesthood. The shutters of the balcony moved slowly apart, and Elder Grandfather Kiv peGanz Brajjyd stood there, looking old and extremely tired.

Kris rose in his stirrups, facing the old priest, and bowed his head. Then he looked up again at the balcony.

"Honored and Ancient Grandfather," he said ringingly, "There is the money which the Earthmen—*stole!*" He waved at the great heap of metal in the middle of the Square.

"We have driven the demons off," Kris said. "I, and the people of Nidor, have rid the land forever of the agents of the Great Darkness."

The old priest could do nothing but stare at the heap of cobalt in the middle of the Square of Holy Light. It seemed to be the only thing in the world for the aged man.

"I see," he said hollowly, still staring at the heap of coin. His voice was so soft that Kris could barely hear it.

"Return the money to the Bank of Dimay," Kris said. "Our savings and our world are safe again. May we have your blessing, Grandfather?"

The Inn of the Purple Deest became Kris' Gelusar headquarters. He established himself there, and began to send feelers into the Holy City, gauging the reaction of the people to the sudden destruction of the School.

The word was good. He was becoming known as Kris

peKym the Exorcist, and, faced with the overwhelming proof afforded by the discovered cobalt, the reputation of both the School and the Earthmen had dwindled to nothing overnight.

On the third day after the burning of the School, the now-famed Hundred Men rode to the Great Temple with Kris at their head. They arrayed themselves around the square while their Captain dismounted and walked alone into the Holiest Temple of the Great Light.

Kris pushed open the giant doors and stepped into the dimness of the Temple. He was alone. There were no other worshippers in the huge auditorium. He stood at the door for a moment, feeling dwarfed by the building's vastness. Then he strode somberly down the aisle between the empty seats, walking toward the Altar of the Great Light.

It was near the hour of Midmeal, the only time of day when the Great Light could actually be seen as a single entity. At that time, the Great Light became a dimly-outlined spot of fire directly overhead. During the morning and the afternoon, the Great Light spread all over the sky; the eternal cloud layer that covered Nidor glowed with His radiance. But near midmeal, His effulgence burned through the sky and illuminated the land beneath.

His Light was focussed through the huge lens in the roof of the Temple, creating a glowing ball of light on the top of the altar.

During the hour, the focus of the light moved slowly across the altar. Kris felt oddly alone in the huge, high-ceilinged room. He paused as he neared the altar, watched the shimmering image of the Great Light.

Have I done right? he asked of the glowing image on the altar. There was no answer.

Kris bowed before the image on the altar and then

seated himself in the front row of seats, those usually reserved for the priesthood. Kneeling in prayer, he waited for the midday ceremonies to begin.

Kris had his eyes on the altar when the priest and his acolytes came in, and he didn't move his gaze. But he watched them with his peripheral vision as the File of Sixteen came from the sacristy to the altar.

He could see that the priest who led the File had glanced out over the auditorium, but it was difficult to read his expression. Was he surprised because there was no one else in the Temple, or was he surprised that there was anyone there at all?

Kris forced the conjecture from his mind and concentrated on the blaze at the altar. In his hand, he held the Book of Liturgy, which dictated the service for the day.

The File of Sixteen arranged themselves before the altar. Each of the sixteen acolytes was arrayed in a different robe; their color and designs represented the traditional patterns of each one of the Sixteen Clans of Nidor. Kris felt a glow of pride as he recognized the red and yellow-green check of the Clan Yorgen at the left of the priest.

Each of the Clans was represented—the Yorgen, the Brajjyd, The Dmorno, the Shavill, the Hebylla, the Sesom, the Nitha, the Vyless, the . . .

He could enumerate every one of them, right down the row. He had thought that the religious training of his childhood had faded completely during his years at sea, but he realized that old Kym, his father, and Elta, his mother, had pounded more into his brain than he had thought.

After a moment of silent prayer, the priest said, "O Great and Holy Light, we pray that the offering we bring to You this midday will be acceptable in Your sight."

He turned and faced the auditorium. He seemed not

to notice that Kris peKym was the only worshipper in the building.

Kris had given careful orders to the Hundred Men. They were not to force anyone away from the Great Temple; they were simply to tell those who came that Kris peKym was inside and wished to be alone. So far, no one had entered, and now it was too late. The service had begun.

The priest was a young man. His voice was strong as he gazed out at the empty auditorium and said, "We have gathered here to perform the Holy Sacrifice to Him Who rules our lives and our destinies."

He raised his arms and crossed them at the wrists. "Let us give our prayers to the Great Light."

Kris knelt and read the prayer from the Book of Liturgy.

"O Great and Brilliant Light let this, our sacrifice to You, be blessed. Guide us, if You will, in the Way of our Ancestors, and the Law of the great Lawyer, Bel-rogas, who was illumined by Your radiance in the days of the Catastrophe which destroyed the evil-doers of the world. Keep us and protect us in the Truth and the Light."

Kris heard the echo of his words ringing in the empty auditorium.

The priest raised his crossed arms again. "May the Great Light illumine you as He does the world."

"And may He guide us in the Way and the Light," Kris responded.

The young priest turned to the altar again. The glowing spot of the Image was approaching the Central Pit.

The sixteen acolytes stepped up to the altar, each one carrying a small bronze box. The priest bowed again to the shining Image and took a large bronze cup from its receptacle on the altar. Then he turned to the acolytes, facing the auditorium again.

"O Shining Holiness," said the priest, "Accept these, the gifts of the Clans, as the Sacrifice which You have ordained."

Each of the acolytes opened his small bronze casket and took a pinch of the powdered herb that it contained. The pinch of powder was reverently placed within the bronze cup held by the priest. Each of the acolytes went in turn, the order of the Clans corresponding to the order of the years in a Cycle of sixteen.

Then the priest held the cup of herbs above his head, faced the great shining lens in the roof, and spoke a brief prayer of offering. After a moment, he turned and placed the cup in the Central Pit taking care not to obscure the light from above, which was moving slowly toward the center.

The young priest again looked out over the empty Temple.

"Who are you who come to pay your respect and worship to the Great Light?"

It was the moment that Kris had been waiting for. He stood, and, reading carefully from the Book of Liturgy, he answered the question, putting his own name in the proper place.

"I am Kris, son of Kym, of the Clan of Yorgen. I come this day to say to the Great Light: I have done wrong, O Holy Light; I have done wrong against Your Law and against the Way of our Ancestors. But I say that I have intended no wrong against You, and I say upon my honor that I will avoid such wrongs in the future. I ask your blessing, O Great Light, that I may never do wrong again."

The priest crossed his wrists in supplication and said:

"You are pardoned for your error in the effulgence of the Great Light."

He turned back to the altar.

At that moment, the focus of rays from the Great Light struck the Central Pit and the cup of powdered herbs that lay within it. For several seconds, nothing happened. Then, the herbs began to smoke, sending a pleasant aroma through the Temple. At last, the powder burst into a green flame. It flickered for nearly a minute, and then died.

The service was over.

14

When he stepped out of the Temple, Kris saw Dran peDran waiting for him. The little Bronze Islander leaned from the saddle of his deest and said, "Captain, Secretary Norvis is come from Tammulcor. He is wait for you at the Inn."

Kris nodded and mounted his own animal, paying no attention to the throngs of people that lined the streets leading to the Square of Holy Light. None of them had crossed the line of black-and-red-clad men who guarded the Square.

Kris signalled, and the Hundred Men fell into formation behind him, following him toward the Inn of the Purple Deest.

Norvis peKrin Dmorno was waiting in the banquet room. He was just finishing his midmeal; across the table from him sat Marja geDel Vyless. The girl saw Kris first, and she stood up with a happy little cry when he entered the room.

Norvis stood too, extending his hand. "You did a beautiful job, Kris. All Nidor is talking about the great Kris peKym who drove the devils out."

"You were wonderful, Kris peKym," said Marja, holding his other hand tightly. There was a light in her eyes that Kris had never seen before.

Kris eased himself into a plush chair. "What brings you here, Norvis?"

The Secretary grinned. "In the first place, we wanted to bask in the reflected light of your glory; in the second, we thought you might need a little money."

Kris returned the grin. "It wouldn't hurt anything. Is there anything left in the treasury at all?"

"There's more than you can imagine, Kris peKym," Marja said. "You've made more money for the Party in a year than my father made in fourteen."

"Donations?" Kris asked.

She shook her head. "Some of it, of course. But most of it is the money you got for us."

"The Dimay scrip," Norvis said. "Since all that cobalt went back into the Bank of Dimay at Tammulcor, the notes that you bought at two for one are now worth their full value. We're twice as rich as when we began."

"Good," Kris said. "We've got quite a bill here at the Inn. It wouldn't bother me in the least to tell the manager he owed it to us, but I think it's better to pay it, as long as we have the cash."

"I'll take care of it immediately," Norvis said.

Kris turned to Marja. "How are things with you?" he asked. "It's a long ride from Tammulcor. Tired?"

"We didn't ride; Norvis brought the *Krand.*"

Kris nodded. "And how's your brother?"

"Ganz is fine," the girl said. "He's really doing things in Tammulcor."

"Just a second," Kris said. "How come you came up on the *Krand?*"

Norvis spread his hands. "How else could we bring a few hundred thousand weights in cash? On deestback?"

"You're right," Kris admitted. "Where's she docked?"

"Number Three Pier. I gave half your crew liberty; they wanted to see Gelusar. I hope that's all right."

"Certainly," Kris said.

"Good. What are your plans now?"

Kris leaned forward. "I've got it all figured out. Actually, we don't know if the Earthmen will ever come back or not. We'll have to make sure that if they do we'll be prepared for them. So I've sent a message to Elder Grandfather Kiv peGanz, telling him that I want to talk to him about the running of the Council from now on. The Merchant's Party should have some kind of voice in the government."

Norvis nodded slowly. "Yes. Yes, I suppose that's best. What did he say?"

"I haven't heard yet; he hasn't replied. I imagine the old gentleman's still a little shocked by what happened to the Bel-rogas School."

Marja blinked at him. "But I thought you were just at the Great Temple. Weren't you seeing him?"

"No," Kris told her. "I went to the midday service. There was no one there but me, and the priest was just a young man. I doubt if any of the Elders will be conducting services themselves until the next feast day."

Norvis rose. "Everything seems to be nicely in hand now. I guess I'd better go back to the *Krand* and pick up a little of our ill-gotten gains. I didn't want to bring it with me until I knew for sure how much you needed."

"Just enough to keep us here at the Inn," Kris said. "A hundred men and deests can eat a lot of food."

"I'll take care of it," Norvis assured him, as he turned and walked out of the room.

Kris followed him out with his eyes and then looked

back at the girl. Just for an instant, he was a trifle startled. She had her elbows on the table, and her chin was cradled in her palms. She was staring at him intently.

"What's the matter?" he asked lightly. "Do I need a bath or something?"

She flashed white teeth in a bright smile. "Something, perhaps, but not a bath. You look very fine—very handsome. You know, you've a very wonderful man, Kris peKym."

Kris smiled a little. "In all modesty, I must admit that you are perfectly correct, my dear."

"Say that again," she said.

Kris shrugged amiably. "In all modesty—"

"No," she interrupted. "Not that part. Just 'my dear.' "

Kris cocked his head to one side. "I do believe that you have something simmering inside that pretty head of yours. Have I been so busy with my work that I've missed something?"

Marja's eyes crinkled at the corners. "Actually, I haven't had a chance to talk to you since I met you. It's been Earthmen, Earthmen, Earthmen. But now that they're gone, maybe you can find time to pay attention to other things."

Kris realized suddenly that he *had* been too busy to see something that had been right in front of him for a long time. "You know," he said slowly, "I think you've got a point there."

Thunder reverberated in Kris' ears. He blinked his eyes open, and the thundering resolved itself into a pounding on the door of his room.

He sat up in bed. What was going on? He'd left two men at the door with orders that he wasn't to be disturbed. He thumbed the sleep out of his eyes and pushed himself out of bed.

"Who is it?" he called.

"Norvis peKrin."

Kris opened the door just a crack. "What in Darkness do you want?" he growled irritably. Then he saw that Norvis was not alone; he was accompanied by Grandfather Marn peFulda Brajjyd, the Priest-Mayor of Vashcor. "Your pardon, Grandfather. I didn't see you. I'll be out in a minute."

He dressed quickly and went out into the hall, closing the door carefully behind him.

The Grandfather and Norvis were both smiling. *No trouble afoot,* Kris thought, relieved. "What is it?" he asked, straightening his vest.

"My blessing," said the Grandfather. "I have a message for you from the Ancient Grandfather, the Elder Kiv peGanz Brajjyd."

"Oh?" Kris said softly. "What does the Elder Grandfather want?"

Marn peFulda clasped his hands on his chest. "You and your Hundred are to appear this morning in the Square of Holy Light, at the Hour of Second Prayer. The Elder Grandfathers will address you then."

Kris folded his arms, a half-smile on his lips. "Do you have any idea what they have to say?"

The Grandfather shrugged slightly. "I can't say, officially. All I was told was that you, Kris peKym, have done something which has come to the attention of the Council, should be given the award you have earned."

Kris repressed the urge to grin happily, "I thank you, Aged Grandfather."

"You're becoming quite an important man, Kris," Norvis said. "I went down to the *Krand* this morning and found that a third of the crew are missing. Evidently, they're having a time of it in town, bragging that they are the crew of the great Captain Kris peKym Yorgen."

Kris smiled. "I'll hang 'em by their feet from the yardarm if they show up too late. After I break open a few kegs of beer, of course. Let's go. Will you come with us, Aged Grandfather?"

Marn peFulda bowed. "I will, my son. It will be an honor."

The Hundred Men rode grandly into the Square of Holy Light. This time, there was no need for them to guard the entrances for their Captain; each of the streets was blocked by Peacemen. Even the Uncle of Public Peace of Holy Gelusar was there, standing importantly just beneath the balcony.

Kris glanced up toward the steeple and saw an acolyte waiting there, mallet in hand.

That's good, he thought. *I won't have to get Dran to ring it this time.* He forced the smile from his face and moved his deest toward the balcony.

The Hundred Men arrayed themselves behind him. From the windows of the buildings that surrounded them, faces peered out, and Kris could see the yellow robes of acolytes of the Temple ranged all around the Square, looking down from the roofs of the surrounding buildings.

Kris stopped his animal just beneath the balcony. Reverently, he bowed his head in silent prayer.

The gong sounded.

Kris raised his head as the shutters of the balcony slid open.

The scene was strangely like that of the questioning of the Earthman—except that Smith was missing.

Otherwise, all was the same. The Elders were clad in full dress; chains and coronets gleamed in the bright morning light. The sixteen old men made an imposing group, there on the balcony.

The Elder Grandfather Kiv peGanz stood up. Looking past Kris, he seemed to glance out over the crowd. He raised his arms, pronounced a blessing, then peered downward almost directly at Kris.

"Four days ago," Grandfather Kiv said solemnly, "a band of citizens, led by Kris peKym Yorgen, stormed the Bel-rogas School of Divine Law, destroyed it, and drove off the Earthmen."

Kris nodded. *Yes, yes,* he thought. *And now they call me up and pin the medal on me.*

Suddenly, the Grandfather said sternly, "Since that time, we of the Council have received additional knowledge about Kris peKym."

There was an odd note in the Grandfather's voice. Kris looked long and hard at the old man, and he felt his lips growing dry. New knowledge about him? What did that mean? How much did Kiv actually know?

Grandfather Kiv peGanz looked down, and for the first time allowed his gaze to rest upon the face of the young man on the deest.

"Kris peKym Yorgen," he said, in a voice that carried loudly across the Square of Holy Light, "We have brought forth proof—absolute and undeniable proof—that you and your men were the ones who robbed the Bank of Dimay, that you and your men buried the metal on the campus of the School of Divine Law. We have uncontrovertible proof that you have committed what is undoubtedly the foulest crime that has ever been done on Nidor.

"Therefore, Kris peKym Yorgen, I order your arrest in the Holy Name of the Great Light—on charges of sacrilege, blasphemy, murder, and high treason! Surrender for trial or die!"

Kris froze for an instant, unable to believe what he had heard. Wildly, Kris looked around him and saw that he had been trapped. All plans were smashed now; the vast and fantastic hoax he had planned had somehow been unmasked.

He glanced up The acolytes and the Peacemen who surrounded the Square had been armed with rifles. At least two hundred firearms were levelled at him from the windows and the roofs of the buildings around him.

"We have you, Kris peKym," said the Elder Grandfather. "Surrender or I'll have you cut down like a peych-bean at harvest time!"

15

"This place isn't fit for broken-down deests!" Kris roared furiously, banging on the door of the cell. No one answered. He listened to the echoing of his voice for a moment, scowled, and kicked the door angrily. "Guard! Guard!"

Again no answer. Kris turned away and dropped miserably on the hard bench running along one side of the cell. "Great Light give me patience," he muttered.

The cells beneath the Great Temple had never been designed for comfort. Normally, the big bronze doors were left open, since the cells were designed for the penitential prayers of erring acolytes, but if it was necessary to close the doors, it could be done.

They were closed now, all of them. The Hundred Men had been jammed in, four to a cell, but Kris had been given a cell all to himself.

After a day and a half in the bowels of the Temple since the unexpected ambush in the Square of Holy Light, Kris was both miserable and furious. He had no food, no one to talk to, not even a decent place to stretch his long legs.

The air in the cell seemed to be about half water vapor; the walls, although only slightly cooler than the steaming atmosphere, were dripping with condensa-

tion. A stream of tepid water poured out of a small pipe
in the back of the cell and splashed endlessly into an
open hole below it, thus providing both drinking water
and sewage disposal. From above, a dim light filtered
down through the tube, and only at midday was there
enough light. The chimney was slanted at just the right
angle to allow the Great Light to hit the floor at midday, so that praying acolytes who occupied the cell
might make their proper devotions.

Kris shook his head at the thought of acolytes
praying down here. How anyone could bring himself to
stay in this dank place voluntarily was beyond him.

"Guard! Guard! Get me some food!"

His voice echoed down into the distance, but no one
came. He had scarcely expected anyone, but he was
determined to let them know from time to time that he
was still down there and angry about it.

But if he was uncomfortable, what must the Hundred
be suffering, jammed as they were four to a cell? Kris
had no way of knowing; the walls were so thick that no
sound had come to him in a day and a half.

He whacked his fist against the bronze door and
roared again. "Are you leaving me to rot down here?"

This time, there was a sound in response—a scraping
at the door that indicated that the bar was being raised.
Then the door swung open. Air that was relatively fresh
drifted in.

"It's about time," Kris snapped.

He watched as two rifle-bearing acolytes filed into
the cell. Behind them came a third man, a young priest
with a cast in one eye and a look of almost intolerable
arrogance about his face.

"Where's my food?" Kris demanded.

The priest chuckled. "Food? Hah!"

The three stared menacingly at him, and for just an

instant Kris thought they were going to execute him on the spot, without even the formality of a trial.

Then the priest gestured and said, "Come along, devil. The judges are waiting."

Kris hung back. "Am I to be tried?"

"It's the custom, before a blasphemer is stoned," the priest replied evenly. "Come, now."

The acolytes seized him roughly by the arms and pushed him to the door. They were small men, and ordinarily he could have flicked them away with two swipes of his hands. But they were armed, and there was little sense resisting. Even if he got away from these three, he'd never find his way out of the Temple alive.

Kris marched ahead of them, down a long, clammy-walled corridor, toward the steep, narrow stairway which led up to the Temple itself. For a while, he nursed the idea of running up the steps and getting away, but he realized that the men behind him could hardly miss, at this range.

As he started up the steps, he saw that they had been thinking a step ahead of him. Another acolyte stood at the top of the stairs, holding one of the three-foot peych-knives that had been taken from his men. He would never have gotten past that.

His face was unsmiling and hard as he strode down the upper corridor toward the main auditorium. Somewhere in the background, a bell was tolling solemnly. Kris didn't like the sound of that.

Once, when he was eight, he had attended a Passing Service in the Temple. It was a mass service, for those killed in the rioting after the Peych Panic, and among those dead had been Kris' parents. He remembered the awe-inspiring solemnity of that service, the far-off shuddering of the Great Temple gong and the low, constant murmur of priestly voices. It seemed to him now that he was marching steadily forward toward his own Passing Service, and the thought was not a cheering one.

He entered the auditorium. As he stepped over the threshold, a ringing voice cried, "Stand where you are!"

Kris stopped and looked up. On a dais at the front of the auditorium, the Council of Elders was arrayed in full panoply; sixteen stern faces glared coldly at him. Along the sides of the auditorium was an assemblage of priests, their blue tunics forming a solid wall down either side of the auditorium. In the center, a small, probably highly select, group of laymen sat quietly.

Two small platforms had been erected at opposite ends of the auditorium, and a fierce light played down from above on each—not the Great Light, but an artificial illumination which hurt Kris' eyes.

One of the platforms was already occupied. A man stood bathed in light, arms folded, staring belligerently at Kris. Kris wrinkled his forehead, wondering where he had seen the man before.

On the dais old Kiv pointed to Kris peKym.

"Show the blasphemer to his station!"

Guards and acolytes bustled around behind Kris, pushing him to the unoccupied platform. He ascended it and stood there, blinking in the harsh light.

"The trial shall now begin," Kiv said.

"Hold it!" Kris said loudly. His voice sounded harsh in his own ears. "Where are my men?"

"Your men are below," said the Elder Grandfather. "It is awkward to have all of them here at once—so you shall stand proxy for all!"

"I see. How convenient."

The Elder Yorgen stepped forward on the platform and delivered a long, rambling, and extremely solemn invocation. Kris listened to only the first few words, then let his attention drift away. He'd heard enough such speeches to know their general tenor.

The matter at hand was serious, though. He was in Grandfather Kiv's hands—and, battered as the Priesthood was, it could still muster enough strength to stone a hundred men quickly and quietly, before the populace knew exactly what was happening. The transition from adored hero to revered martyr would be a quick one.

Kris frowned. Was there any proof that he, Kris peKym Yorgen, had actually led the onslaught? In truth, he hadn't—he'd merely brought the people there and shown them the buried money. They had done the rest unbidden.

And this business of proving that Kris had planted the money at Bel-rogas. Could it be done? Kris knew his men were loyal; none would testify against him. In any event, the accusation was too fantastic to be credible, even though it happened to be true.

Then he stiffened. Did the Elders *need* proof? All they had to do was to put up a reasonably convincing prosecution and hustle Kris off the scene quickly. They could do to Kris what Kris had done to the School—act first, answer questions later. Come what may, there was no more School now. Perhaps the Elders were figuring the same way—come what may, at the end of the trial there would be no more Kris peKym.

"The trial will now proceed," Grandfather Kiv said suddenly. Kris snapped his head up. "We charge you, Kris peKym of the Clan Yorgen, of blasphemy, murder, and sacrilege! How do you answer this charge?"

"I answer that the charge is false!" Kris declared. "Totally false!"

"We shall see," Grandfather Kiv said. "Let us hear the witness."

* * *

A priest came forward to the other small platform, stood in the glare of the light, and recited something to the mysteriously familiar man who stood there. The witness for the prosecution, Kris thought. *Who is he?*

Probably someone bribed to denounce me, he thought bitterly. *Kiv doesn't miss a move.*

They had him neatly penned, all right. Like a fool, he had walked straight into their ambush, and now they had him. Would his death crush the movement? He didn't know. Norvis was still at large someplace, and Ganz peDel—but could they carry on alone?

The priest finished administering the oath to the man in the testimonial box, and returned to his seat. Kiv, from the platform, said, "Stand forth and speak, Bryl pePrannt Hebylla!"

Of course! Kris recognized him then. It was Bor pePrannt's brother, who had been with Bor when the two of them had tried to hold up his office that day—so long ago!—when he was changing money.

"Tell the Council what you know, Bryl pePrannt," the Elder Grandfather said.

"All I know, Ancient Grandfather, is what my brother told me. But my brother is innocent, Ancient Grandfather; he only did what this man—" He indicated Kris—"told him to do. He didn't know there was anything wrong."

"Never fear, Bryl pePrannt," the Elder Grandfather said. "Your brother will be freed."

So that was it! That was the dirty, filthy, underhanded trick they were playing—letting Bor go free on the condition that Bryl talk! Kris felt his muscles tighten and his stomach seemed to be a cold lump within him.

"Well," Bryl said, without looking at Kris, "on the fourth night after the Feast of the Lesser Light, my brother was with this man on board his ship, the *Krand*. They came up to Gelusar with the cobalt hidden in a false bottom of the ship. They went overland from the bend in the river south of Gelusar and took the money to the Bel-rogas School—"

"Mourn its holy name," a lesser priest intoned.

"Yes—uh—" Bryl seemed a little confused by the interruption, but the eyes of the Council were still on him. "Anyway, they took the cobalt and buried it on the school grounds and then came back to Tammulcor."

"Excellent," Grandfather Kiv said.

"Just a minute!" Kris shot to his feet. One of the acolytes standing nearby raised his peych-knife, but a signal from the Elder Grandfather stopped him.

"This man is a thief and a liar!" Kris shouted angrily. "What evidence do you have to back up this ridiculous story?"

"The evidence will be shown," Grandfather Kiv said coldly. "We have witnesses who saw the *Krand* come upriver with many deests on its deck—but we know that the ship never arrived at Gelusar. Also, we have the ship itself—and the double hull has been found. That, I think, is enough to substantiate the story Bryl pePrannt tells."

Kris felt as though he had been slapped in the face. The *Krand* captured?

"Do you call that evidence enough to stone a man?" Kris asked loudly. His voice was still as firm as ever.

"It is," said Grandfather Kiv. "It is, and more than enough. But we have still more." He turned toward his left and called out: "Bring in the other witnesses!"

A group of acolytes appeared, bringing with them four men—members of Kris peKym's own crew. Kris sat down slowly.

The Elder Grandfather addressed the four crewmen. "As you have been told, it is no crime to follow the orders of your captain. Indeed, to fail to do so is mutiny. But it is one thing to commit a crime because you were ordered to do so, and another to comply freely with the act. To fail to testify here would indicate that you condone your captain's actions, that you deserve the same death as he does—stoning.

"Your testimony, however, will indicate to us that you were merely following orders and are therefore innocent of any crime. Will you testify?"

The sly snake! Kris thought. Loyal as they might be, what else could they do in a situation like that but spill everything? A bath of cold perspiration spangled his forehead as he saw now that there was no way out for him whatsoever.

The answer of the four was pure formality. It was obvious to Kris that they had already decided to tell the Council what had happened.

They did. One by one, they climbed into the testimonial box and told their stories. This time, unlike Bryl's testimony, they were questioned for detail. They gave detailed and explicit answers.

Kris could see the whole pattern. Bryl had come to Gelusar somehow—maybe he had blabbed what Bor had told him—maybe he'd thought he could get paid—maybe a lot of things—

And the shrewd old man had used Bryl's worthless, undocumented testimony to club the crewmen into giving testimony that was far from useless. It clinched the case against Kris peKym Yorgen perfectly. Like a meat-deest being led to the butcher's, like a peych-stalk under the farmer's knife, Kris peKym would be put to the stones.

When it was all over, the Council conferred for a few minutes. Then Grandfather Kiv peGanz Brajjyd rose ominously and said, "Have you anything to say before sentence is given, Kris peKym Yorgen?"

Kris stood up slowly. "Yes, Elder Grandfather, I do." He turned and looked at the hushed crowd in the auditorium. "The Council will condemn me to death. I will die for what I have done. But let me tell you this: they have condemned me because they are still under the influence of the devil Earthmen, the demons of the Outer Darkness. They condemn me, but I do not condemn them—they have already condemned themselves far beyond anything I could do or say."

Then, as the crowd began to whisper, he turned back to the Elder Grandfather. His hand jabbed out in a sharp gesture. "And I tell you, Elder Grandfather, that for this day's work, the Great Light Himself will condemn you even more than you have already condemned yourself."

"I stand ready to assume responsibility for my deeds," Grandfather Kiv said. "May the Great Light deal with me as I deserve, if I have erred this afternoon." He drew his robes solemnly about him. There was a long, tense, crackling moment of silence.

"Kris peKym Yorgen, we, the Elder Grandfathers of the Sixteen Clans of Nidor, in Council assembled, find you guilty of the multiple crimes of sacrilege against the property of the Great Light, blasphemy against the Great Light, and high treason against the governors appointed by the Great Light. As the Law of our Ancestors dictates, you and your men shall be stoned to death at firstlight tomorrow. We speak in the Name of the Great Light."

The blazing twin lights from above winked out suddenly. The trial was over.

16

Norvis peKrin Dmorno brought his deest pelting up the road toward the Great Temple, and reined the animal up and tethered it near the Temple wall in the Square of Holy Light. He dropped off, tired, and leaned against the panting animal's side for a moment.

It had been a hard ride, down to Tammulcor and back—but it had been necessary, in order to save Kris peKym. Norvis had made the journey to the southern port in what must have been record time, despite the nuisance of having a deest die under him on route.

Outside the Temple, he encountered a boy passing by, and stopped him. "Tell me, boy—how did the trial of the blasphemer go today? I've only just arrived from Tammulcor."

"Found guilty, Old One," the boy said. "Guilty and sentenced to die at firstlight tomorrow. The trial just ended a few minutes ago."

"Thanks," Norvis said, and walked on without bothering with the formalities. He entered the Square of Holy Light and looked around. The place was deserted, here in the dim light of late afternoon.

Firstlight tomorrow, eh? Quickly he computed the various spans of time. It had been a little more than a day and a half since Kris had been captured; a little less than a day and a half since Norvis had made his mad ride to Tammulcor to rouse Ganz peDel and the army.

Ganz and his men would be coming up the Tammul as fast as they could make their obstinate ships move; they would be in Gelusar in a few hours—certainly long before the scheduled time of the execution. In the meantime, Norvis knew he would have to move quickly.

The trial, Norvis thought, had ended not unexpectedly. Kris was a menace to the Council, and they were happy to be rid of him. Norvis paused on the first step of the Temple, planning what had to be done.

Kris was too important to lose. As a focal point for the rebellion, he was indispensable to the Party. And therefore, steps would have to be taken to save him. Norvis fingered the pistol concealed in his robe and slipped silently into the quiet Temple.

An acolyte stepped forward in the half-darkness.

"May the Great Light illumine your soul," the acolyte said, in ritual greeting.

"And yours," Norvis said crisply, averting his face. "I am here to pray." He indicated a small chapel to the left.

"Very well," the acolyte said.

Norvis entered the chapel. A small lens glittered above. He bowed his head, but no prayers would come. After a few minutes, he rose and looked around warily. No one was in sight.

No one had seen him, either, but the one acolyte—and in this darkness, he would not be recognized. Wrapping his tunic around him, he edged out of the chapel and toward the darkened staircase.

There was the sound of close-harmony chanting in the distance as Norvis tiptoed up the stairs toward the private office of Elder Grandfather Kiv peGanz Brajjyd.

* * *

Norvis knocked once, lightly, and there was no reply. *The old man doesn't hear too well any more*, he thought, and knocked again.

"Come in, come in!"

Norvis pushed open the door and stepped through. The old man was sitting behind his desk, glaring steadily in the general direction of the door. It was evident that Kiv's sight was none too good either.

It was hardly surprising. Norvis himself was close to forty; Kiv was probably more than twice his age. The pistol under Norvis' arm suddenly began to burn coldly against his flesh.

"The Peace of your Ancestors be with you, Grandfather," Norvis said.

"May the Great Light illumine your soul, my son."

Norvis stepped closer and bowed. "My name is Norvis peKrin Dmorno, Grandfather. I know I'm not of your clan, but—"

"What is it you want?" Kiv asked impatiently. "How did you get here unannounced? You're one of those Merchant people, aren't you?" Irritably, Kiv began to rearrange papers on his cluttered desk.

"That's right, Grandfather. I'm here to ask for the release of our Leader, Kris peKym Yorgen."

"*What!* Here to plead for the life of a condemned blasphemer!" Kiv was fiery, animated now. "Out! Away from me!"

"Just a minute, Grandfather Kiv peGanz," Norvis said quietly. He felt almost numb, now as he watched the silver-bodied Elder rage at him. "Don't be hasty, Grandfather. You know what the Scripture says about haste. 'He who—' "

"Out!" Kiv stormed. "Guard! Guard!"

The gun at Norvis' side was like a stone strapped to his body. He took three quick steps forward and laid his hand lightly on Kiv's wrist.

"Do you remember your daughter, Ancient One? Sindi iRahn Brajjyd?"

"Eh?"

"*Your daughter—your daughter had a son, Grandfather.*"

The inflection of that last word was unmistakable. Kiv turned, stared dimly at Norvis for a moment, pulled his arm from the other's grasp, and sat down, staring at his fingertips.

"Grandfather?"

"My name is Norvis peRahn Brajjyd," Norvis said. It was the first time he had uttered those words in almost fifteen years, and they sounded strange in his throat. "Do you remember me, Grandfather?"

Kiv seemed to grow even more shrivelled as Norvis watched. His lips moved uncomprehendingly. Finally he said: "Norvis peRahn was stoned to death fourteen and more years ago."

"Norvis peRahn escaped. Norvis peRahn dove into the waters of Shining Lake and fled down to Tammulcor, where he climbed back into his convenient alias of Norvis peKrin Dmorno—under which colors he's been riding ever since."

Kiv let the words sink in. "But why?" he asked blankly. "Why have you hidden your name, your—" He shook his head. *"Are* you Norvis peRahn?"

Norvis folded his arms. "I entered the Bel-rogas School of Divine Law some twenty years ago, the fifth of my family so to do. The first was someone named Kiv peGanz Brajjyd—and his wife, Narla iKiv. My mother and father both were students there. I too hoped to graduate from the School, and continue my work in genetics. Unfortunately—" his lips curled bitterly—"I became, instead, the first student ever to be expelled from Bel-rogas. Does this sound like your defunct grandson, or doesn't it?"

"It does," Kiv admitted. "But—"

"But why? Because I'd be dead for real if I hadn't hidden my true identity. Who do you think was responsible for selling that growth hormone all over Nidor?"

"Norvis peKrin—Norvis peKrin and the other one, the sea captain. And all the time it was you?"

"Exactly. We were duped by the Earthmen into distributing the stuff widely."

Kiv shook his head bewilderedly. "But—why have you come here, Norvis?" He seemed still unable to comprehend the fact that his grandsom could still be alive after all.

Norvis walked around behind the desk and put his arm around the withered old man. "I've come to warn you against your mistakes, Grandfather."

"Mistakes?"

"You've placed your trust in the Earthmen, Kiv peGanz. I did too—for a while. Until Smith betrayed me, and I learned the Earthmen are devils come here to destroy Nidor."

"I've heard those words before," Kiv said softly.

"You've never thought about them," Norvis said. "Let me illumine your mind, as the timeworn expression goes. Let me scrape some of the scales from your eyes."

"Harsh words from a young man," Kiv said.

"We're past the point of formality now, Grandfather. Listen to me—*listen*, for the first time in your eighty years. Listen!"

"Very well," Kiv assented. There was little fight left in the old man now. "I'll listen."

"Do you remember my expulsion?" Norvis asked.

Kiv nodded. "I wish I could forget it."

"And I. It nearly killed my mother, and the stain of it is still on the Brajjyd name. Do you know *why* I was expelled?"

Kiv searched his memory. "Some scene you made at a public ceremony, wasn't it?"

Norvis nodded. "I had been studying genetics under Smith, the Earthman. After a year of hard work, I had developed a growth hormone. With the connivance of the Earthman, the invention of the hormone was credited to a thoroughly worthless young man named Dran peNiblo Sesom—long since deceased."

"What happened to him?"

"He was lynched when the hormone he supposedly invented wrecked our economy. It was a fate I escaped, through the good offices of the Earthmen, who were kind enough to heave me out of the school and put the credit—or blame—on Dran peNiblo."

"You say you were expelled falsely?" Kiv repeated. "I believe you raised that charge at the time."

"And how often have you heard it since, from men thrown out of the School for no good cause? The Earthmen have been following some mysterious plan of their own, Kiv peGanz—one that necessitated my expulsion. They're secretly working to destroy Nidor!"

"You and your friends have said that many times," Kiv objected. "You used it as an excuse to steal cobalt, plant it on the Bel-rogas grounds, and destroy the School—a crime for which your hotheaded young friend will die tomorrow."

"Kris will not die," Norvis said.

"Is that the Light's Truth?" said Kiv sarcastically.

"It is. You will free Kris to continue the fight against the Earthmen."

"The Earthmen are gone," Kiv said.

"They are not gone. *They are hiding in the Mountains of the Morning, biding their time.* Once you've removed

156

Kris from their path, they will reappear—and destroy us all!''

"Hiding? What madness is this?''

Norvis grasped the old man's arm—*dry, like an old stick*—and peered into his deepest eyes. "Remember, Grandfather, when my mother Sindi crossed the Mountains of the Morning, following my father, Rahn?''

"I remember," Kiv said.

"She returned—after a slight delay on route. In the Mountains of the Morning, there is a secret place where the Earthmen stay. Sindi saw strange and wonderful things there—the strangest of them being the Earthman Jones, supposedly gone to the Great Light some time before.''

"Jones?" Kiv was openly incredulous. "How do you know all this, boy?''

"Sindi told me of it," said Norvis. "Of the Earthmen and their strange machines and weapons, out there in the Mountains. I have never forgotten it.''

Kiv put his head in his hands. "I'm old, Norvis. I don't understand all these conflicting stories. What are you trying to tell me?''

"I'm trying to tell you," Norvis said, "that the Earthmen have been aiming for Nidor's destruction ever since they came here. That the students of the School have been carefully trained to sow havoc among us. You with your well-meant method for wiping out crop-eating pests, that caused a mild panic sixty years ago—and incidentally helped to put a large-sized crack in our social framework. Me, with my growth hormone. You can almost detail the step-by-step way in which the Earthmen have undermined us.''

Kiv said nothing, but merely closed his eyes wearily.

"The Earthmen are still here," Norvis continued relentlessly. "Waiting to perform some new wickedness. And by taking Kris peKym from us, you'll be removing the last obstacle in their way."

Kiv opened his eyes suddenly. They glinted beadily at Norvis. "How do I know what you say is true?"

"Will you *never* believe anything?" Norvis demanded, exasperated. "I swear that all I've told you today is as true as that book you see there"—he indicated the Scripture and the Law. "I swear by the honor of my mother, Sindi iRahn, by my father, by the Scripture and the Law, by my true name of Brajjyd, by my Ancestors, and by the Great Light Himself that I have not lied to you. I—"

"Enough!" Kiv said hoarsely.

His face was pale, and Norvis saw that the old priest's breath was coming in heavy gasps. "For sixty years—ever since my days at the Bel-rogas School—I have cooperated with the Earthmen. Not since my days at Bel-rogas have I doubted the rightness of what I have done—and my doubt was only momentary."

Kiv seemed to sag. "And yet," he went on, "if what you say is true, then *I* have done more to aid the Earthmen than any other single man." His head slipped lower. "I have betrayed my people and my world—if what you say is true."

"Can you still doubt me?"

"I don't know," Kiv said. "Your oath—but—"

"Free Kris peKym!" Norvis said inexorably. "Free him!"

"Norvis! How can I?"

"Free him!"

Kiv rose from his seat and wiped trembling hands over his brow. A tremendous inner struggle seemed to be going on in him.

"You *couldn't* have lied to me, Norvis. And yet—"

"Face the truth, Kiv peGanz!"

Kiv stood still for a moment. Suddenly, he uttered a little moan and slumped to his seat, his head falling forward over his desk. He moaned again—once—and was silent.

Norvis caught his breath. It hadn't been necessary to use the pistol, after all. It was just as well this way.

He glanced down at the body of the aged priest. For just a moment, a tear glistened at the corner of Norvis' eye. Angrily, he wiped it away, and started for the door.

There were footsteps in the hall, and then a tapping at the door. "Ancient Grandfather?" a voice said.

Norvis stopped, cursing himself for a fool. It was the first time in fifteen years that he had exposed himself to physical danger, and here he was, in a jam again.

"Ancient Grandfather?" Again the knock—louder this time.

Lightly, Norvis ran to the window and looked down. Below was the roof of the auditorium, and in its center was the great lens that focussed the rays of the Great Light on the altar. Across from him was the gong tower. The wall was carved intricately; Dran peDran had been able to climb it easily.

But Dran peDran was a younger man; Norvis hadn't climbed the rigging of a ship for—by the Light! It was nearly twelve years! He realized suddenly that he had become middle-aged. His muscles were flabby from years of sitting behind a desk.

"Ancient Grandfather!" A pounding on the door.

There was nothing else he could do; if he were caught, everything—*everything* would be ruined! He swung himself over the window sill and began to work his way down the carved wall. He was less than ten feet down when he heard the door open in the Elder Grandfather's office.

Someone, an acolyte probably, came into the room. Below, Norvis hugged the wall.

"Grandfather? Grandfather! *Grandfather!*" A silence for a moment, then the fast patter of retreating sandals.

Moving as rapidly as he dared, taking advantage of the late afternoon dusk, Norvis went on down the wall. He dropped the last few feet, wincing as the shock of hitting the ground flashed through his legs, and ran across the roof toward the rear of the Temple. He felt a touch of panic, hard to suppress. There was still a chance he might be caught.

He swung himself over the edge of the roof, and, for a moment, his feet touched nothing. Then a sculptured gargoyle came within reach. He grasped its grinning head and eased downwards. His fingers slipped, and he dropped nine feet to the street below.

His legs took the second shock poorly; his ankles felt sore from the wrench they had been given. But he didn't dare limp. Gritting his teeth, he walked quietly down the deserted street to the corner, and then turned and walked to where his deest was tethered. His face a wooden mask that concealed searing pain, he hoisted himself aboard the animal.

He turned it toward the south, moving slowly so as not to attract attention. As the deest began to move, he heard a sudden shout behind him.

"He is dead! The Elder Grandfather is dead!"

Norvis glanced around. It was not an acolyte who shouted; it was one of the lesser priests, standing at the door of the Temple.

Then the great gong sounded—and sounded again. Norvis urged his mount forward, and the deest trotted quickly through the Square of Holy Light toward the south. And as he rode, through the night-darkened streets, Norvis peRahn Brajjyd heard the gong ring hollowly again and again over the Holy City, sounding the death knell of his grandfather.

17

Once out of the city, Norvis took the Tammul Road toward the river; the ships from Tammulcor should be coming in any time now, commanded by Del peFenn's son, Ganz peDel. The ships would have to be stopped. Things had changed now—and, much as Norvis hated himself for thinking it, changed for the better.

He had gone up to the old man's office to do murder, if necessary—and found that he couldn't, and that it hadn't been necessary. He knew he could never have pressed the trigger on the old man. A fool old Kiv peGanz had been, but he had been an honest fool—and honesty, while it was not a trait Norvis could claim for himself, was one that he respected.

Norvis pulled up at the turn of the road at the great arch of the Bridge of Klid. There was only one way he could stop Ganz's fleet. The river was over a mile wide at this point.

He guided his mount toward the bridge. At the far end, there would have been Peacemen a few days ago, but now that the cobalt had been recovered, the bridge was free again.

Norvis went to the center of the bridge and waited, hoping that the ships would be visible in the glow of orange spread by the torches on the bridge.

A few deest-mounted men trotted by, paying no attention to the man who stood by his mount and stared downstream toward the south. Pedestrians plodded by, some silent, some talking in low tones. All Gelusar and the country surrounding seemed to be hushed.

One man, obviously more than a little drunk on peych-beer, stopped by the rail of the bridge near Norvis.

"Did you hear? The Elder Grandfather is dead. Not too long ago. The old man was wrong, I guess."

Norvis glanced at him and then looked again downstream. The nightly rain had begun by now, and he felt cold and chilled.

"He said this morning," the drunk continued, "that if he was wrong about Kris peKym, the Great Light would kill him. And now he's dead! Bet *he* was surprised!"

Norvis turned to him again. "Keep a civil tongue, you souse, or I'll take great pleasure in throwing you into the Tammul with an anchor to keep you company!"

The man blinked. "All right, all right. Sorry." He went on across the bridge.

It was another five minutes before Norvis saw the masts of the *Vyothin* sliding toward him in the darkness. The ship, he saw, would pass under the bridge fifty yards away. Norvis urged his deest along the bridge.

Without paying any attention to whether or not there was anyone watching, he climbed over the rail and hung by his hands from the bracing beams of the mile-long bridge. Just as the *Vyothin's* mast passed beneath him, he let go and dropped toward the arm of the main skysail. He grabbed it. The sail was moist from the night rain, and his hands slipped a few inches,

162

but he held on, nearly wrenching his arms out of his shoulder sockets. Then, slowly and painfully, he began to climb down the rigging toward the deck.

The man in the crow's nest had seen him, of course. He sung out: "Who's there? Who was that just dropped?"

"Me," Norvis called weakly. "Norvis peKrin Dmorno. Tell Ganz peDel I'm here."

Several minutes later, he was in Ganz peDel's cabin.

"I'm getting old," Norvis said, smiling a little. "Ten years ago, I could have done that without taking a deep breath."

Young Ganz peDel shook his head. "I'm sure *I* wouldn't have done it. Kris peKym might have the nerve, though."

Norvis shrugged one shoulder. "No matter. The point is, we've got to get Kris out of the Temple—and I think it's going to be easier than we thought."

"I don't understand how the Grandfather's death changes anything," Ganz peDel said. "All we have to do is get our men inside the Temple, as if we were praying. Then someone can sneak down—"

"Hold it, son. You're forgetting something. The Elder Grandfather specifically stated, in public, that if he had erred the Great Light would deal with him. Well, He has."

Ganz nodded. "I get it. The people now are going to realize that Kris must have been right all along. We won't have to sneak; we can attack the Temple openly!"

"Right. Absolutely right. But it also means we'll have to stir up popular support. That's why I had to stop you—if you'd just charged in there, you might have gotten Kris out, but it wouldn't have endeared us to the people. This way, we'll have the people on our side before we make a move."

"Good," said Ganz happily. He stopped pacing the floor of his cabin. "By the way, how is Marja?"

"Why—I suppose she's all right. She was at the hotel when I left yesterday, and I haven't been by there since." Norvis looked up at Ganz blankly. "Why? Are you worried about your sister?"

"Not really. She can take care of herself."

"Right enough," said Norvis. He paused and sat up straight. "Wait! What's that?"

Ganz frowned a little. "I don't—oh, yes—"

From somewhere just ahead of the ship came the sound of a peculiar, angry, buzzing murmur. Both men scrambled up the ladder to the deck.

Norvis reached the deck first and peered out, looking around. At Gelusar, the Tammul River widens into the Gelusar Basin before it narrows again to flow on to Tammulcor and the sea. At that point, the Tammul is nearly two miles across. On the western side of the river, where Gelusar lay, were the docks for the river packets and the other vessels that came up from the south.

The *Vyothin,* followed by the *Paleth* and the *Garn,* had sailed into the Gelusar Basin and moved toward the docks. The *Vyothin* was less than five hundred yards offshore as Norvis and Ganz came on deck. There were torches blazing on the dock, and a huge crowd was gathered there, screaming and shouting.

"What in the name of—what's going on?" Ganz asked.

"Looks like a gathering of some kind," Norvis said sarcastically. "Maybe a garden party."

"Or a riot?"

"Or a riot," agreed Norvis. "Better move in slowly; we don't want to get caught in anything nasty."

The *Vyothin* drifted westward toward the docks.

Soon, the men on deck could make out what was happening. Norvis could see someone standing on one of the high pillars facing one of the docks, and the crowd was cheering.

"The *Vyothin!* Hoy! Hoy! And the *Paleth!* And the *Garn!* Hoy! Hoy!"

And then the figure on the pillar waved its hands, and a familiar voice rang across the water.

"Yes! Here they come, just as I told you! The devil-influenced Elder is dead because the Great Light killed him for condemning Kris peKym to die! And now his friends—your friends—*our* friends—have come to rescue him from the dungeons!"

"Hoy! Hoy! HOY!"

Ganz turned his head to look at Norvis. "By the Rays of the Light," he said softly. "It's Marja!"

There was little need to stir up popular support for the rescue of Kris peKym Yorgen. The news had spread quickly over Gelusar that the Elder Grandfather was dead, and Marja geDel Vyless had taken advantage of it by telling everyone that it proved Kris' innocence, and that his friends would come to get him out of his dungeon. She had known that Norvis had gone after her brother, and had estimated the time of arrival pretty closely. When the ships pulled in, she had already organized a full-fledged army, ready to march on the Temple to demand the release of Kris.

Norvis and Ganz were the first men off the ship. The crowd looked ugly, but Marja seemed to have them under control. Her face was positively radiant with fury, love, hatred, and joy—a bower of emotions which seemed to flicker across her face as though they were competing for domination. Norvis hadn't realized a woman could look like that.

She pointed a finger at them. "There they are! I told

you they'd come! Are you ready to save the Blessed Kris from a martyr's death? Are you ready to save him from the minions of the devil-influenced Elder whom the Great Light has struck dead for his unrighteousness?"

The cry rose from a thousand throats. *"Yes! Save him! Save him!"*

Norvis tried to push his way through the crowd and shut the girl up. The crowd gave way, but not rapidly enough.

"Once before," she went on, "the people of Gelusar rallied against evil and drove off the Earthmen! Tonight, we must rally and cleanse ourselves of the last vestige of evil!"

There was more cheering. Norvis jabbed viciously to the right and left with his elbows and finally got through to her. The thing might get out of hand. He wanted to rescue Kris, but not quite this way.

But before he could say anything, Ganz had taken his sister's hand. "Marja," he said softly, "you're magnificent! You reminded me of Father up there!"

"It wasn't Father I was thinking of," she said. "It was Kris. I didn't know if you'd make it or not, and I wasn't going to let him die."

Norvis stepped back and let some of the tenseness seep out of him. It was too late. Events would have to move of their own accord for a while, until they could be brought back under control.

Ganz turned and looked at him. "On to the Temple?"

"On to the Temple," Norvis said. "Where else?"

Ganz lifted his head and shouted through cupped hands to the men on the ship. *"Hoy!* Hoy, aboard ship! Get your weapons out! Down and off! The people of Gelusar are with us! Let's march!"

18

The acolytes and priests at the Great Temple of Light were not unprepared for what was to come. They had heard the rumors that had flitted through the city in the last hour or two since the Elder Grandfather had been found dead, and they remembered all too well what had happened to the School of Divine Law.

The doors of the Temple were barred; there were men on the roofs and stationed in the towers, armed with rifles, and there were men on the lower floors armed with great knives, ready to defend the Temple against any onslaught.

Nor were the priests the only ones who were prepared to fight for the Holy Ground. Citizens from everywhere who had heard of the uprising gathered in the Square of Holy Light. They had not heard Grandfather Kiv's fulfilled curse on himself; they knew only that the Temple was under attack.

When the mob surged into the Square, they met armed resistance. Hands locked together, the townfolk blocked the way. Peych-knives swung, rifles coughed from the roofs. Men dropped, bleeding and dying.

And still the invaders of the Square swarmed in

through the three streets that led to it. Those who were in front were pressed ever onward by the relentless masses behind. Within fifteen minutes, the Square was slippery with blood, and the dead and dying were stumbling blocks for those who still fought—and as yet the Temple had not been touched.

Norvis, Ganz and Marja were elsewhere. Norvis had finally persuaded the young hotheads that a frontal attack on the Temple, although it would be useful as a diversion, would not be the most direct way of releasing Kris. While the battle raged in the Square, the crews from the ships worked their way around to the rear of the Temple.

"Let's keep it quiet, men," Ganz said. "We'll come up from behind. They'll never know what hit them."

At the rear of the Temple was a narrow street, the same one down which Norvis had fled not too long before. It was watched by the priests; there was no chance of simply walking up that alleyway and taking the Temple easily. But Norvis had a plan.

A block to the rear of the Temple, he pointed to a two-story business building. It was dark, but in the gloom they could see a sign that read:

EGIL & peMEGIL
FINE POTTERY AND DISHWARE

"The back of this building faces on the rear of the Temple," Norvis said. "Ganz, you take a group to the roof and get the priests' minds off the alleyway below. You'll be one floor above them, so you'll have an advantage. They'll have to look up to shoot, so they won't be watching us. The rest of us will get through the window at the rear of the pottery shop and take the rear doors of the Temple."

With the butt of a rifle, Norvis smashed in the door

of the shop and the men surged in. Dishes and vases were scattered as the men plunged into the blackness of the pottery shop.

One of them struck a torch and held it aloft. He pointed toward the back of the store. "There's the stair to the top!"

The torchlight glittered on broken fragments of blue and red and gold and green glazeware that lay in shards on the floor.

"Watch that torch!" Ganz said. "Put it out before we get to the top, or they'll spot us! *Vyothin* men, come with me! The rest of you follow Norvis peKrin!"

Ganz headed for the stairway, followed by the crew of the *Vyothin*.

"This way, you others!" Norvis commanded. "And watch that pottery! Do you want to wake up the whole neighborhood?"

The men laughed, relaxing a little. The battle that still surged back and forth in the Square of Holy Light would drown out any noise that the crewmen could possibly make.

Norvis led them to the rear window. It was shuttered, and Norvis slid the bolt. "Now be quiet. I mean it, this time. If the priests suspect we're down here, we're lost. They know by now that we're in this building, but since there's no door, they won't be looking down here unless we're too noisy. So shut up."

He eased the shutter open a crack and looked up.

"What's going on?" someone said.

Norvis jerked his head around. "Marja! What in the name of Darkness are you doing here? Get back! This is men's work!"

Marja said a single sharp, vulgar word. "If you think I'm going to stand around and do nothing, you're wrong. You can tell Ganz what to do, but you'll not keep me from Kris!"

Norvis wavered for a moment. He could order the men

to take her back, but that would only create confusion. He cursed softly, then said: "All right. You stay. I'll treat you like a man—but you'd better obey like a man. Is that clear?"

"Yes, Old One," she said crisply.

By this time, Ganz and his men had reached the roof. There was a rattle of rifle fire, which was immediately returned from the roof of the Temple. Then, for a moment, there was silence.

Norvis gritted his teeth at the stupidity of Ganz's men and Ganz himself. The dumb sons of deests had all fired at the same time, a broadside into the priestly ranks. It had undoubtedly been effective—but now they had to stop and reload, giving the priests a breather that staggered fire would have averted.

Oh, well. Some men could reload faster than others. It would even itself out shortly.

The men behind him were growing impatient, but there was nothing Norvis could do but wait. Soon, the fire from the roof of the pottery shop began to form into a staggered pattern. And then Norvis heard an odd sound. It was a regular *thump! thump! thump!* that echoed around the streets that led to the front of the Temple.

It was drowned out for a moment by a loud, clarion ring from the Temple gong as a bullet struck it.

Then Norvis recognized the thumps. The mob at the front was battering at the door. He'd have to move fast.

He turned to Marja and whispered, "You and I will go first. We'll jump out of the window and run across the alley to the rear door of the Temple. If your brother keeps up the good work, no priest will dare lean over and try to shoot us. Don't try to get inside yet, though. Wait till I tell you." Then he flung open the shutter. "Let's go."

They leaped and ran. Not a shot was fired downward

until long after Norvis and Marja were safe beneath the wall.

Meanwhile, the others were streaming from the window. It was less than thirty feet across the street, and the first few men made it safely. Then a priest saw them from above, and began firing at the window.

Three men dropped, one after another.

"There's enough of us here!" Norvis called. "The rest of you go upstairs and help Ganz!"

Then he turned to the men around him. "We're going in this door," he said. "There are probably men behind it, but if the main doors are being assaulted as heavily as it sounds, there won't be very many. All of you aim your weapons at the door. When I push it open, wait for my signal, and then fire."

He reached into his vest and pulled the heavy pistol from his belt. There was only a small bolt on the door; the Temple hadn't been built with the expectation of an armed assault.

Norvis stared at the door. Once, many years ago, he had been taken into the Temple through it by a friend of his mother's, Yorgen peBor Yorgen, whose father's father had been the Elder Yorgen. Norvis had only been ten at the time, but for some reason the fact stuck in his mind that the bolt had been at Yorgen peBor's shoulder height.

He lifted the pistol, pressed it against the door, and pulled the trigger. The resulting explosion almost tore his arm off.

"Hoy!"

He had never tried that trick before, and he had no idea of what pent-up gases from exploding gunpowder could do. His hand was numb, and the pistol was ruined, but the door swung open of its own accord.

There were two acolytes in the narrow hallway

Waving his useless pistol, Norvis ordered harshly, "Shoot them!"

The acolytes had just enough time to look startled before bullets ripped into them. The small group of sailors moved on into the darkened hallway, heading toward the dungeons. At the front of the Temple, the frantic assault continued noisily.

19

In the blackness of his unlighted cell, Kris peKym Yorgen stood just beneath the air chimney that led to the roof of the Temple, his head cocked to one side to catch the sounds that drifted down from above.

What in the Name of the Light was going on up there, anyway? An occasional *crack!* of rifle fire was recognizable, but the murmuring and rumble in the background was hard to make out.

A mob again? It didn't seem likely. With all that damning evidence marshalled against him and his guilt proven beyond doubt, it wasn't likely that any of the people would still be on his side. The people all knew he had framed the Earthmen; why would they help him now?

The idea that Norvis might be storming the Temple to rescue him seemed just a little fantastic, but it was the only explanation he could think of. If it were Norvis, he thought, then there wasn't much chance of a rescue. A surprise move might have done it, a quick lightning swoop—but it sounded as though the populace had been aroused, and, if so, the few remaining loyal members of the Party would not last long against their fury.

He cursed bitterly. If only he could get out of this son-of-a-deesting cell!

He heard noises reverberating faintly through the bronze door, and whirled quickly. If there were someone coming to rescue him, the priests might think it wisest to kill him now, instead of waiting until morning.

He walked quickly to the door of the cell and felt around. The cell was just narrow enough for what he wanted to do. A shorter man might not be able to manage it, but Kris thought he could.

Bracing his feet against one wall and his shoulders against the other, he began working his way up the rough stone wall. Once he was above the door, he turned and put his back against the wall over the door, keeping his feet and shoulders against the side walls. He was ready for anyone who came in. Die he might, but at least one priest would go down with a broken neck.

The noises in the hall were faint, but they kept up. And still no one opened his door. *What's going on?* Kris wondered again. His shoulder and leg muscles were tiring rapidly. By the time he finally heard the bar of his door being lifted, he was so cramped that he was ready to drop.

The door swung outward. There was a discordant burst of sound, as though there were many men in the hall, and a blaze of torchlight glittered in the room. Kris poised himself to leap.

"Kris?" a voice said. "Kris, are you in there?"

Kris said: *"Marja!"* Between the cramping of his muscles and the surprise of hearing her voice, he lost his brace against the walls, toppled outward, and collapsed in a heap at the girl's feet.

He stood up gingerly, grinning. "I guess nothing's

broken," he said, rubbing his leg. He glanced around at the group who had filed into his cell. "What's happened?"

She told him quickly. "And when we got down here, we couldn't find which cell you were in. We've released all the other men."

"Good going." He glanced at Norvis, who stood behind Marja holding a torch. "Let's get the men together and get out of here."

The news had been good—astonishing, even. So the Elder Grandfather was dead? Didn't that prove that the Great Light was on the side of Kris peKym Yorgen?

"Up the stairs!" Kris yelled. The men followed him out of the dungeon level and upward. Just as they emerged on the top of the stairs, a tremendous crash echoed through the building, followed by the savage roar of a raging mob. The doors of the Temple were down!

"Out the back way!" Kris snapped. It was a good feeling to be in command of his men again. "That mob's blind. It would just as likely kill us as anyone!" He charged down the hall with over a hundred men at his heels. There was a priest in the hall, but at sight of them, he dropped his peych-knife and fled wildly.

There was no one firing from the roof as the men poured out the back door. Ganz peDel was at the window of the pottery shop.

"We were about to come in after you," he said. "The priests who aren't dead have deserted the roof and gone below!"

"Stand aside!" Kris called. "Open those shutters wider! We're coming through."

It took time for a hundred-odd men to get through the window, and more of Megil & peMegil's pottery went the way of all dishware, but it was no more than a few minutes before the operation was completed. Kris pulled the shutters closed and bolted them. "Up to the roof," he said. "Maybe we can see what's happening."

From the roof of the pottery shop, there was little to see at first. There were unmoving blue-and-yellow-clad figures lying scattered over the roof of the Temple, but there was no sign of life. They could see the far edge of the Square, but it was difficult to tell whether there was anyone moving in the flickering torchlight.

But the roaring screams of the frenzied mob still filled the air.

Suddenly, one of Kris' men shouted, "Look! Look at the lens!"

The great lens on the roof of the Temple was glowing with orange-red light.

"Torches," someone said.

Kris shook his head. "Torches? No! Those damned silly fools are *burning the Temple!*"

It was true. The glow beneath the lens became brighter, and the howl of the mob changed in pitch and character as they ran out of the building, trampling their way back over the fallen front door. Soon the Square of Holy Light was filled with fleeing people.

Kris felt the way he had felt when the School had burned—helpless. But it was worse this time. He had not wanted to fire the Great Temple—no, not the Temple.

"The lens! The lens! Look at it!" Kris realized it was his own voice shouting.

A black fissure was moving across the huge lens, spreading rapidly, flawing its perfection. Then another and another appeared. The cooling rain dropping on it from above was competing with the hellish fire beneath.

Then, with a sudden roar, like a crack of thunder, the

four-thousand-year-old lens, which had brought the beams of the Great Light into the Temple for hundreds of generations of Nidorians to worship, shattered into fragments and collapsed into the inferno of flame below.

20

Leader Kris peKym Yorgen stopped at the gaping door of the Temple and looked in, as he had every morning for the week since the Temple's destruction. Norvis, at his side, waited patiently.

The interior of the auditorium was a blackened ruin. The costly drapes, the intricately carved pews, the fine panelling were nothing but ash which lay soggily on the floor, wet by the nightly rains that poured through the opening in the roof that once had held the lens. Now the hole gaped openly like a raw wound. Somehow, Kris felt that he had lost a part of himself when the Temple burned. The Bel-rogas School had been nothing, actually. A century ago, it had not even existed.

But the Temple had stood for four thousand years, rock-solid and seemingly eternal. And now it was a gutted shell.

Only the interior of the auditorium had been burned; the thick stone walls of the building itself had only been blackened from holding the flames until they burned themselves out. The offices and the meeting rooms were untouched.

"You keep looking at that, Kris," Norvis said softly. "Are you thinking of cleaning it up, or rebuilding it, or—?"

Kris shook his head decisively. "No. Not yet. Not until the Council has been re-formed and we've returned to the Way of our Ancestors. Only then will we be worthy of rebuilding the Temple. It was desecrated by the Earthmen and the Great Light has cleansed it with fire."

He turned toward the side door of the Temple, leading into the offices and business rooms. The bronze doors that led into the auditorium had been discolored and warped by the heat, but they had held back the fire.

The guard at the stairway nodded as they approached. "Hoy, Ancient Leader. Hoy, Aged Secretary."

Kris nodded curtly and ascended the stair to his office. Norvis followed him.

Grandfather Marn peFulda Brajjyd was already waiting in the outer office, his fingers rubbing the small lens that hung on a silver chain around his neck. "Bless you, Leader Kris."

"And you, Grandfather. What brings you here so early?"

"I've appointed a new Priest-Mayor of Vashcor," Marn peFulda said. "An excellent young man. And as the oldest living priest of the Clan Brajjyd, I've come to take my place on the Council."

"Fine!" Kris said. "Let's go inside my office and figure this thing out."

"Your Announcement of Purification was a great stroke, my son," the Grandfather said as he followed Kris into the inner office. "It saved the life of a good many priests. Perhaps even I might not be alive today if you hadn't told the people that all those who were still under the influence of the Earthmen were dead."

They entered the office. Norvis said, "I'll go to my own room, Kris. I have a great deal of work to do."

Kris nodded. "Go ahead. There's plenty to be done." After Norvis was gone, Kris waved the priest to the chair facing his desk. "Sit down, Grandfather. We've got a little figuring to do. Nidor is still in an uproar. I've put the whole world under Peace Law—my men are acting as Peacemen, with the regular Peacemen under them. But that's not the Way of our Ancestors. We must return to the Way."

The priest nodded without speaking.

"There are nine of the original Council left alive after the fire," Kris said. "With you, that makes ten. We're six short."

Marn peFulda nodded. "And with the records destroyed, we have no way of actually knowing who the oldest priests of each Clan are. It may involve a little guesswork before we've filled the Council again, and—" he paused and smiled slyly—"I don't know *how* we'll ever decide who the Elder Leader will be."

"It doesn't matter," Kris said decisively. "We'll fill the Council somehow. And—you are hereby appointed Leader of the Council yourself, until the emergency's over. You'll take rank over all present and future members. They'll obey your orders."

"Excellent," the priest agreed. "It's a drastic measure, I'll admit—but these are times that require drastic measures."

"Right. There are a few other things to take care of, too. The old Council found me guilty of sacrilege, treason, and blasphemy. Ah—that decision must be set aside, since the Great Light has shown that I was right."

"Naturally," said the priest smoothly.

"There's only one other thing. Technically speaking, I hold no position in the Government at all. I think it might be wise to see to it that I have some sort of official standing."

The old man's eyes narrowed in thought. "There's no office I know of that—wait a minute!" He stood up, walked to the bookcase in the back of the office, and took down the Scripture and the Law.

He flipped the sacred volume open, riffled through the pages, and selected the passage he wanted. "Here it is. Seventh Section. 'And it happened that in the days of Dmorno the Holy, the Great Light sent a blight over the land, for the people were unrighteous. The clouds that shielded the world from His angry radiance were dissipated and became thin, and the crops were withered and great storms raged. Being without food, the people suffered greatly.

" 'Now, at that time there lived a man of great wealth in Gelusar who had stored away vast quantities of peych-beans for his own subsistence, and the Council declared that he had much more than he needed, and that food from his warehouses should be dispensed to the poor and the needy. This he refused to do.

" 'Thereupon, the Council appointed an Executive Officer, a pious and strong man named Lordeth, who was given command of Peacemen and who went forth to the rich merchant and took from him his warehouses and distributed the food therein to the people.' "

The priest closed the book. "There you are. In emergencies it is perfectly proper to appoint an Executive Officer." He frowned. "I hope I can get the Council to agree."

"They'll agree," Kris said cheerfully. "If they don't they'll wish they had. We *must* return to the Way of our Ancestors!"

The priest smiled. "You'll be the first man to hold that office in three thousand years, Kris peKym. You have a great responsibility, my son."

In a nearby office, Norvis fingered a writing pen in his hand as he spoke to little Dran peDran Gormek.

"Now, do you follow me, Dran peDran? Not a word of this to anyone."

Dran fidgeted. "Not even to the Captain?"

Norvis pursed his lips. "Kris doesn't want it known that he even suspects there still are Earthmen on Nidor. It would weaken his position, you see. If I'd selected anyone but you for the job, I'd have told them that Leader Kris doesn't even know about it. But I can trust you. Never even mention to him that you know anything about this—understand? That's the way he wants it."

Dran nodded. "I doesn't quite understand, but if the Captain says so—he says so."

"Very well, then. Now look at the map." Norvis indicated a map of Nidor hanging on the wall. "Here's Gelusar. Due East are the Mountains of the Morning. Here—" He made a tiny cross with his pen—"is the Earthmen's base. You'll go by deest to the foothills of the Mountains of the Morning, and then climb on foot the rest of the way. Now, mind you: all you're to do is look over the base. You're not to expose yourself in anyway. Keep out of sight and you'll be safe."

"I'll do, sir."

"I want to know how many Earthmen there are, and whether it would be possible for us to get at them if we moved carefully. Perhaps they won't even be there; they may have deserted the base. But make sure, and don't go into the base itself, even if it looks deserted. Understand?"

"I understands," Dran said. "I goes immediately?"

"Immediately," Norvis said.

The small Bronze Islander left without further word. Norvis waited for him to close the door, then leaned forward and clasped his hands on his desk, looking abstractedly at the inlaid pattern in the wood.

The threads were beginning to come together now. Kris had proven to be three times the leader Del ever was—and the School lay in ruins, the Temple was a husk, Kiv was dead, and the power of the Council broken. Nidor's downward slide had been checked—maybe.

The whole thing hinged on whether the Earthmen were actually gone or not. Norvis' mother, Sindi iRahn peKiv Brajjyd, had told him about the base when he was young. His father, Rahn peDorvis, had run away from the Bel-rogas School for some reason—Sindi had never said why—and Sindi had followed him. Rahn, taking a shortcut across the mountains on his way to Vashcor, had stumbled on the Earthmen's lair, and Sindi behind him. Rahn had been caught, and by some mysterious magic had had all memory of his visit removed. Sindi, unobserved, had seen all.

Norvis knew his mother had told the truth; the base was out there. It presented a potential threat to Nidor as long as it remained. How could they proceed with the job of rebuilding, if the Earthmen might be still on the planet?

Norvis needed information. Dran, a trained seaman, was observant. He should be able to bring back plenty of information. *And it's information we need,* Norvis thought grimly. *We don't know nearly enough about the Earthmen—yet!*

21

Kris peKym looked out his window over Holy Gelusar and frowned. He had driven the Earthmen from Nidor; he had purified the Council. But the emergency was not yet over; he had much yet to do.

His attention was distracted by a motion at the corner of his eye. It was someone mounted on a magnificent blue-gray deest, trotting across the Square of Holy Light.

He smiled as he recognized Marja geDel. She deserved a magnificent deest; she was a magnificent woman. The rifle-armed guards around the Square nodded deferentially as she passed, giving honor to the betrothed of the Leader. Kris smiled. He hadn't asked her yet, but there was no question about it.

Or was there? Come to think of it, he'd better make sure. His position on Nidor would be just that much more secure if he were a family man.

The girl cantered her animal across the Square, dismounted before the Temple, and tethered her deest. She hadn't looked up. It would have been undignified for her to wave at him, or for him to call to her. She entered the door below, disappearing from Kris' sight.

He returned to his desk and sat down. Within less than a minute, there was a rap at the door.

"Come in, Marja."

She opened the door, smiling radiantly, and closed it again behind her. "Do you have any more work for me this morning?"

"Yes, as a matter of fact, I do. Sit down a minute."

She frowned in puzzlement at his brusque manner. Kris ignored the expression, pulled a piece of paper toward him, and began writing.

"Kris—"

"Wait till I've finished, Marja."

He wrote deliberately, clamping his lips. When he was through, he lifted his eyes and handed her the paper. "Take this list into the market center first. Have the stuff delivered if you can't carry it. That last item you'll have to look for—but don't take anything less than the best."

She read through the list. "All kinds of clothing—and furniture—and—and a *house!*" She looked up. "Kris what *is* this?"

He rested his chin in his palm and grinned at her. "If you're going to be Marja iKris, you'll have to have the best of everything, won't you?"

"Oh, Kris! When?"

"Three days is the proper time after announcement, isn't it? I'll announce it today."

"Fine," she said happily. "You'll have to ask Norvis peKrin first, though."

"Norvis? Why Norvis?"

"Didn't you know? Father signed guardianship of Ganz and me over to Norvis in case of his death—he did it several years ago."

"No, I didn't know that," Kris said. "But do you *need* a guardian? You're old enough to know what you're doing, you and your brother."

"Nevertheless, you'll ask Norvis. This has to be done properly."

"Anything you say. You'll have both him and Ganz as escorts, then?"

She smiled. "I think that would be the best. While you're talking to Norvis, I'll see to this list. But I'll need money."

"Don't worry about that," Kris said expansively. "Just tell the merchants to collect from Norvis, that's all."

She leaned over the desk and kissed him before she left.

It was more than the customary three days before the marriage could take place. On the scheduled wedding day, four more priests turned up with claims for the Elderhood, and each of them had to be considered in turn by the Council. Annoyed, Kris postponed the wedding two days and presided over a hearing, Marn peFulda at his side.

Two of the priests turned out to be of the Clan Shavill, and the younger of the two had to be sent back to his village with regrets. That left three vacancies in the Council: The clans Nitha, Sesom, and Gormek. Rumor had it that a Grandfather Gasus peNils Gormek was going to sail soon from the Bronze Islands, but so far there was no sign of him.

Also, by a solid vote of acclamation, the thirteen Elders decided to appoint Merchants' Party Leader Kris peKym Yorgen as Executive Officer of Nidor, the investiture to take place on the day of the Feast of the Sixteen Clans, which fell a day after his revised wedding date.

The wedding itself was a simple affair, held in the little Temple of Kivar on the southern side of the city. The Elder Grandfather Marn peFulda Brajjyd officiated.

The temple held only a few. The Council Elders attended, and a few personal friends, but the streets were blocked off by Peacemen to prevent the curious gawkers from interfering.

Norvis and Ganz stood on either side of Marja, who was dressed in the traditional purple cloak of maidenhood. Behind them was the altar, before them the open door of the temple. Kris stood in the doorway, resplendent in the black-and-red uniform of the Hundred Men.

Off to one side, Grandfather Marn gave a signal, and Kris strode toward the altar. Four paces before the trio, he stopped and said: "Norvis peKrin Dmorno, Ganz peDel Vyless, I greet you. I come to declare my love for the woman you have sworn to protect."

"Will you swear to protect her as we have?" Norvis asked.

Kris' answer was a long and involved oath, which he couldn't remember and had to read from the Book of Liturgy. When it was over, Norvis said, "If she will accept your oath, we will relinquish claim."

"I accept him," Marja said.

"Then we charge you, Kris peKym, to take her and feed her and clothe her and protect her. She is yours."

Marja stepped forward, and, as she did, Grandfather Marn raised his hand. "Hold! I ask both of you—have you asked the Great Light's blessing on this union?"

"We ask your blessing now, O Ancient Grandfather," Kris said. "And we ask that you pray for us."

Grandfather Marn gave his blessing and the ceremony was over.

It was over, and Norvis, for one, was glad of it. He watched Kris ride off on a deest with Marja in the saddle in front of him, while the Hundred Men led them on a triumphal parade to their new home.

Norvis felt a warm glow of accomplishment as he watched them round the corner and head northward. Kris had done his job and done it well; he deserved what he was getting—wealth beyond any ordinary person's dreams, and one of the most beautiful girls on the face of Nidor.

Quite a triumph, Norvis thought, *for one who would have been a simple peasant's son had all gone well with Nidor.*

Norvis shrugged and mounted his own deest. He had other work to do. He, too, trotted northward, but by a different route; he had no desire to take part in the parade. As he wended his way through the streets, no one seemed to pay any attention to him. He was a non-entity, a nobody, merely the Party Secretary. Which was just the way he liked it.

He was only a few blocks from the Temple when he saw a familiar figure turn onto the avenue from a side street just ahead.

"Dran!" he called. "Dran peDran Gormek!" He urged his mount to a faster pace.

Dran reined in and turned his head. "Hoy! Secretary!"

Norvis pulled up beside him. "How was the trip?"

"I is dirty and tired," Dran said. There was a grin on his owlish face. "Climbing mountains is hard work. I is got good news for you, though. I find—"

"Not yet," Norvis interrupted. "This is too public. You can tell me what you know about *them* at the office."

"But that's just it," Dran said, still grinning. "We isn't got anything to worry about! They isn't there!"

Norvis jerked his head around. "What? What's that?"

"They isn't there," Dran repeated. "I find the place

you mention—a wide, flat area. But there isn't anything there. No buildings, no magic machines, no nothing."

"I see," Norvis said slowly. "Yes, I see."

"That means the Captain really is driven them off Nidor! We is free—really free!"

Norvis nodded abstractedly. When they pulled up in front of the Temple, he said, "Since you found nothing, Dran, there's no need to tell anyone of my foolish suspicions, is there? We'll just forget it."

"Sure, Secretary," Dran agreed. "You is done the right thing. You has to know the truth. Now we knows."

"That's right, Dran. I'll see that you get a bonus for this—and you can do a little celebrating."

"Hoy*hoy!* Thanks to you, Secretary Norvis!"

An hour later, Norvis was saddling his deest and slinging two saddlebags of supplies over the animal. He had told Kris that he was going to Tammulcor on business, to check on the Bank of Dimay, which was still in the throes of reorganization.

But he had no intention of heading south; he was going east, to the Mountains of the Morning. Dran peDran had seen nothing—but that meant nothing. Norvis recalled his mother's telling him how the Earthmen had taken a part of his father's memory. Rahn peDorvis had never remembered anything about that trip to the mountains.

If the Earthmen could take a memory away, couldn't they replace it with a false one?

Maybe there was nothing up there; maybe there never had been. But Norvis realized he could never take another's word for that. Dangerous jobs could be delegated, sure—and, Norvis thought, it was best for all that dangerous jobs be done by someone else. But there were times when a job could only be done by one person—and in this case, that person was Norvis peRahn Brajjyd.

He pushed a pair of pistols into his belt and lifted himself into the saddle. Twenty minutes later, he was trotting across the Bridge of Gon, heading eastward across the Tammul into Thyvash, towards the Mountains of the Morning.

22

The day of the Feast of the Sixteen Clans brought a brisk wind from the east, heavy-laden with dampness.

Kris looked out the window of his office, watching the lower wisps of the eternal cloud blanket scudding across the sky.

"I hope we're not in for a storm," he said. "This would be a poor time for the Great Light to send His Flashing Emissaries across the sky." He smiled grimly. "The noise they make might drown out my speech."

Elder Grandfather Marn peFulda chuckled. "The investiture takes place immediately after the midday services, and the sky ought to be quiet by then. Don't worry about it."

Kris turned from the window and settled himself in his chair. "You know, Grandfather, it's a peculiar feeling to realize that more than four thousand sacrifices have been made to the Great Light on the Feast of the Sixteen Clans at the Great Temple—and this year there will be none."

"I know," the priest agreed. "It is His will."

Kris stared at the surface of his desk for a long moment, and then pulled himself out of his introspective mood with some effort. "You'll be the celebrant at the services, of course?"

The Elder Grandfather nodded. "We'll start at the Temple of Kivar, just as we did with your wedding—but this will be an official ceremony, and, if I may say so, much more imposing. The actual investiture will take place on the balcony of the Great Temple, as you asked."

Kris nodded. "Good. You—"

There was a rap at the door. "It's Ganz peDel, Leader," came the voice.

"Come in, Ganz," Kris called out. He was getting to like the boy; except for the hatred for the priesthood that his father had instilled in him, young Ganz' might eventually have made a good Party Leader. Perhaps, even yet—

The boy walked in. "There's a priest to see you, Leader." There was no distaste in his voice; he had learned to conceal it well. Or perhaps he was actually changing his mind about the priesthood.

"Who is it?" Kris asked.

"A Grandfather Gasus peNils Gormek, of the Bronze Islands."

Elder Grandfather Marn peFulda stood up. "The Gormek Elder! Excellent! Send him in, my son."

Ganz stepped back, closing the door.

Grandfather Marn turned to Kris. "This makes fourteen! The Elder Council will soon be complete, my son. I hope he's as good a man as his predecessor, Elder Vesol peSkel Gormek; in spite of the fact that he was—ah—under the influence of Darkness, he was a wise old man."

Kris shrugged. "Darkness take Vesol peSkel; let's see what this Bronze Islander is like."

The door opened, and a blue-robed priest stepped in. His face was like a piece of wrinkled leather, covered with sparse silvery fuzz. He peered around the room with bright, clear eyes, seeming to take in everything at a glance.

He nodded his head at the Elder Grandfather. "Elder, I asks your blessing. I is Grandfather Gasus peNils Gormek."

Marn peFulda gave his blessing. Then: "May I ask the date of your birth, Grandfather?"

The priest smiled. "On the ninth day after the Feast of the Great Lawyer, in the Year of Dmorno, of the 320th Cycle."

Kris sat up in his seat. The old Gormek was older than Marn peFulda—and theoretically deserved to be Leader!

But the old priest raised his hand. "You doesn't need to worry, Elder Grandfather; I is heard about Leader Kris peKym's order. You is the Elder Leader, and I does not wish to make any claims. I is an old man; I knows nothing about governing a world. I is been isolated on my Islands for more than seventy years. I has no political ambitions, but when I is called, I comes." He turned to Kris. "I gives you my blessing, Leader Kris. You is been needed on Nidor."

Elder Grandfather Marn peFulda relaxed visibly. "I welcome you, *Elder* Grandfather Gasus peNils Gormek. Will you be ready to take part in the investiture of our Executive Officer after the midday services?"

"I is happy to," the Elder Gormek said.

Marn peFulda looked back at Kris and said, "The Council is about to meet. I'll be with you at the services."

Kris nodded. "Good. I'll see you then."

Kris peKym Yorgen, Executive Officer of Nidor, stood upon the balcony of the Great Temple and faced the throngs of people in the Square of Holy Light.

The investiture ceremony was over; a long triumphal procession through the streets had preceded it, with the people cheering on every side.

The procession itself had been colorful. Half of the Hundred Men were in the lead, their red-and-black uniforms worn proudly; the other half brought up the rear. Between them, mounted on brightly caparisoned deests, had come the new Council of Elders, with their blue-and-gold robes and their bronze coronets gleaming in the filtered light. And then, surrounded by yellow-robed acolytes, had come Kris peKym Yorgen, the Great Exorciser and Executive Officer on Nidor.

All this was a bright memory in Kris' mind as he stood on the balcony of the gutted Great Temple and looked at the cheering throng below. Out of the corner of his eye, he saw Elder Grandfather Marn peFulda Brajjyd stand and raise his crossed arms in a general blessing. The crowd became quiet.

The Grandfather looked at the sky. "O Holy Light, we have, this midday, offered our sacrifice in Your name, and now, we ask Your blessing on Your people and on Your Priesthood.

"Led by those who had fallen under the influence of the accursed Earthmen, we have erred in Your sight. But now we have been illumined by Your light, and we seek to repair the damage that has been done and atone for the injury we have done You. We pray for Your blessing upon us."

He lowered his arms and looked out over the Square of Holy Light. "We, the Elders of Nidor, in Council assembled, have come this day to invest in a great man the powers of a special Office. All of you know what has happened—"

The Grandfather continued his introduction for several minutes, but Kris' attention drifted. He thought of what he was going to tell the people. What he said today would not only be spread all over Nidor, but would ring through history for all eternity. It had to be just right. It had to be perfect.

So intent was he on his own thoughts that he barely noticed when the Elder Leader put the bronze chain around his neck—the chain carrying a specially struck medal signifying his office. He scarcely noticed as the other Elders gave him their blessing. Only when the Elder Leader said, "—and now your Executive Officer will speak; I charge you to pay strict attention to what he has to say," did Kris return fully to his surroundings.

He stepped forward to the rail of the balcony and raised his hand to still the shouting and applause.

When the crowd finally grew quiet, he said, "Bless you for your righteousness, my friends. The Great Light has granted us His illumination, and the—"

He got no further. He saw what had happened only a fraction of a second before he felt it.

Across the Square, from a window of one of the buildings, had come a puff of smoke, which the wind had quickly whipped away. Then had come the sound of a loud cough.

And then had come a painless shock, as though someone had hit him hard in the chest with a pillow. Kris fell back, more with surprise than anything else, looking down at the tattered hole in his vest and the blood that seeped out of it.

There was confusion all around him, but still he didn't pay any attention. Someone grasped him by the shoulders and eased him to the floor of the balcony. Someone shouted for a surgeon and a physician. From somewhere came the crack of rifles. But to all these, Kris paid no attention.

He put his hand up to his chest, and someone pulled it away.

"Is he dead?" asked a voice behind him.

"No," said another. "He's badly hurt, but it didn't strike his heart."

"We must get a doctor—quickly!" said a third.

And then sight and sound and feeling dissolved into the darkening blur of unconsciousness.

23

Norvis peRahn Brajjyd wanted to snarl and curse, but he hardly dared breathe. The wind-whipped night rain had made his bodyhair cling soggily to his body, his clothes were dripping with water, and the rocks were so slippery that it seemed almost impossible to climb them—especially with the wind sweeping down the mountains, tugging at his clothing and splashing rain in his eyes.

Still he pushed on; he didn't want to be caught on the mountain when firstlight came. He had waited at the foot of the towering pile of bare rock until nightfall. His mother had climbed it successfully at night, and that was the way he was going to do it.

He knew he was in the right place; it was the only place that looked as though it might be a gap in the mountains through which one could reach Vashcor.

At last he reached the top, and was overjoyed to see the oddly-shaped rock his mother had described to him. Now he knew beyond doubt that he was in the right place.

He edged his way up to the rock and peeped over.

And a vast disappointment washed over him, hardly

diluted at all by the faint sense of relief he felt.

There was nothing there at all. There was nothing but the broad, flat area that Dran peDran had described. It was obvious that there *had* been buildings of some kind here once—the flat plain itself was artificially levelled.

But it was empty. Nothing moved on it, nothing but the little rivulets of water that skittered across its surface ahead of the driving wind.

The Earthmen were really gone, then. Somehow, it didn't seem right. There seemed to be something left unexplained.

"Welcome, Norvis peRahn Brajjyd," said a soft baritone behind him. "I thought you'd never get here."

Norvis turned slowly. The only surprise he felt was in the fact that he was not surprised at all. He knew who it was, and it seemed right somehow.

"Hoy, Smith," he said. He drew his gun and aimed it at the Earthman's midsection. "Wet out, isn't it?"

Smith, standing tall and solid a few feet away, pretended not to notice the gun. "Wet? Yes; I've always hated Nidorian weather. But then, I doubt if you'd like Earth. Direct light from the sun wouldn't be too good for your skin."

Norvis looked at the man he had hated for so long, and felt an almost overwhelming desire to press the trigger. But he stayed his hand. He needed information first.

"What *are* you, Smith?" It was a short, hard question.

"You tell me," the Earthman replied.

"You're mortal, I'm sure of that. You may have long life, but if I shot you, you'd die like anyone else."

The Earthman smiled a little. "Right. And where do we come from? The Outer Darkness?"

"Something like it," said Norvis. "Without the

mystical rot. My guess is this: according to Scripture, a cataclysm thousands of years ago all but wiped out life here. If you read between the mysticism, you'll see that what happened was that most of the great continents sank beneath the sea. Only sixteen families survived to come to Nidor, led by Bel-rogas Yorgen. But I think there are other continents out there in the sea, and I think you Earthmen come from one of them. None of our ships has ever sailed out far enough to find it; they couldn't carry enough food or water. But with the machines you have, you could come to Nidor. Originally, we must have come from the same stock—but men, like animals, can change over the years and diverge from each other. So, in a way, you *are* from the Outer Darkness."

Smith chuckled. "Very clever. Wrong, of course, but very well thought out. I tell you in all truth that we are both from the Outer Darkness and from the place where the Great Light is."

Norvis shrugged. "You're being ridiculously cryptic, but—no matter. What I wanted to ask was—*why?* Why did you have me thrown out of school? Why did you lie? Why did you wreck my life and the life of Nidor?"

"Why? To save your life, Norvis. Remember what happened to Dran peNiblo Sesom?"

Norvis nodded slowly. Dran peNiblo, the snivelling blockhead who had received the credit for discovering the growth hormone Norvis had worked so long and hard to find—Dran peNiblo had been mobbed and hanged because his discovery had caused the Great Depression.

"If you had taken credit for your work," the Earthman went on inexorably, "you would have died as surely as he did. Didn't you ever wonder why such a stupid, mean little creature was ever allowed to enroll at Bel-rogas?"

Norvis blinked. "You let him in just to use him as a scapegoat?"

"Why else? He was expendable—you weren't. And

did we really ruin your life? You've been wealthier, happier, and more powerful this way than if you'd been hailed as the discoverer of the Growth Hormone."

"So poor Dran peNiblo was framed for death. You're a pack of ruthless scoundrels, Smith!" His finger tightened on the trigger, but he didn't quite press it—yet.

"So now it's 'poor Dran,' is it?" Smith asked, sardonically. "And we're ruthless scoundrels? You're thinking isn't very clear tonight, Norvis peRahn. Are we more ruthless than you? Who was it who murdered the man who had befriended him and given him a good job when he was a youth without a weight to his name? *Who was it who shot down Del peFenn Vyless in cold blood?*"

Norvis' gun hand shook. How had the Earthman known that? How did they know so much? How—? He clamped down on his whirling thoughts.

"I did it for the good of Nidor," he said harshly. "Do you think I *liked* doing it? If Del had gone on with his tirades against the priests, the Merchants' Party would have collapsed in a year. He would never have stepped down peacefully and let Kris peKym take over. I had to do it—don't you see?" His voice became almost pleading at the end.

"We *do* see, Norvis. But we want you to see, too. Now do you know how we felt when they hanged an innocent boy? *Now* do you know how we felt when the students and priests of Bel-rogas were butchered by a howling mob? We could have stopped it. We knew the cobalt was buried there. Do you think Kris could have carried off such a stupid trick if we hadn't helped him?" Smith smiled. "We knew what would happen, and we didn't lift a finger to stop it—because it was for the good of Nidor."

For the first time, Norvis thought he saw a glimmer of light. "How?" he said. "Why?"

"Why? Now that you've lowered that pistol, I'll tell you."

Norvis looked at his gun hand. The pistol was pointed at the wet rock at his feet. He brought it up again—and stuck it in his belt.

"All right," he said. "Let's hear it."

Smith's bearded face broke into a grin. "Not here; you must be soaking wet."

"It's nothing. I—" And then, for the first time, he saw that Smith, standing there in the driving rain, was comfortably dry. The raindrops, now that he looked closer seemed to be going *around* the Earthman somehow.

He suddenly felt very foolish. "The bullet would have done the same thing," he said aloud.

Smith nodded. "I'm afraid so. I didn't think you'd shoot, but I value my life very much." He reached inside the pearl-gray shirt and took out a small, flat box which had a belt attached to it. "Put this on," he said, handing it to Norvis. "It's a remote-control job, connected to my own; I'm afraid you couldn't handle the controls without practice."

Numbly, Norvis strapped on the little force-field generator. Smith did something with the box at his own waist, and Norvis felt himself suddenly surrounded by a warm *thickening* of the air around him.

"We're going up," said the Earthman. "Don't panic."

"I won't," Norvis said. Suddenly the ground dropped away from beneath him. He had no sense of motion; it was as though Nidor itself were falling away. He gasped. It was more frightening than anything he had ever felt.

"Relax," Smith said. "Don't look down. Look at me."

Norvis forced his head up. There was Smith, just standing there—with nothing below him. It was as though they were still on the ground.

"It's a little surprising the first time," Smith said. "But you get used to it."

"But—" There was something missing. "Where's—where's the blue glow?"

"This?" Smith touched his belt, and the familiar blue aura surrounded him for a few seconds. Then it blinked off.

"I see," Norvis said. "It isn't a necessary part of the machine's effect; it was just to impress us."

"Partly," agreed Smith, "but it was more to mislead you. If you Nidorians had thought we could float around in the air unseen, you'd have been constantly on the lookout for us at night. But as long as you expected a blue glow, we could do our snooping unsuspected and undetected."

A sudden fog enveloped them, and Norvis felt as though he were hanging suspended in nothingness. "Where are we going, Smith?" His voice sounded strangled and helpless.

"Hold on, Norvis. We're going through the cloud layer."

Suddenly, above him, Norvis saw a glow of light. It seemed to be moving toward him, brightening as it came.

"And what's *that*, Smith?"

"Just the open door of a spaceship," the Earthman said. "The men inside are guiding us toward it now."

They were floating just outside it. It was an open door in a wall of metal—hanging in the sky.

And then he and Smith were floating inside. The door closed behind them, and abruptly everything was all right again. He was standing in an ordinary room—well, all that metal and the queer things around the walls were strange, but it was a room—just a room. Not the terrifying nothingness he had just experienced. He stamped on the floor, enjoying the solid feel of the plastic-covered metal floor beneath his feet.

"Don't rock the boat, Norvis peRahn," said one of the Earthmen, laughing pleasantly.

Norvis looked at the two other Earthmen in the room. "Boat?" he said blankly. "Is this a boat?"

"Something like it," said Smith. "Norvis peRahn, I'd like you to meet my friends, Harrison and Davis."

Norvis nodded mutely. The Earthman Davis looked very much like Smith; Harrison's skin was darker, and he was beardless.

Then he noticed that the Earthmen were looking at him closely. "What's—the—matter?"

Davis and Harrison grinned. "Sorry," Davis said. "We've just never seen a Nidorian in the flesh before. You're a very handsome people."

"They're the crew of this small ship," Smith explained. "They've never seen the populated parts of Nidor, only the spacefield."

Norvis let out his breath. "Can I sit down?"

"Sure," Harrison said. He touched something on the wall, and a small, cunningly-concealed seat slid out. Norvis sat down gratefully. "You call this a ship," he said. "The idea of a ship that sails through the sky is fantastic!"

"Think so? How would you like to see the Great Light?"

In spite of himself, Norvis felt a tingle of shock.

"Before we do," Smith went on, "I'll explain what the Great Light is. It's simply a huge ball of incandescent gas."

"*It?*" Norvis had never heard the Great Light referred to with a neuter pronoun.

"It's a great ball of gas," Smith continued. "So big

that your mind may have trouble grasping it, and so distant from Nidor that it's unbelievable. If there were a road leading from Nidor to the Great Light, and you had a fast deest that would never tire, and you rode at top speed, day and night—it would take you more than a thousand years to reach it!"

Norvis said nothing. He couldn't.

"Take her up, Davis," Smith said. "We'll show him what we're talking about."

A few moments passed, as Norvis sat dazedly. Then Smith said, "Norvis, come here." He walked over to where the three Earthmen were standing in front of a large pane of black glass. Behind the glass were thousands of tiny sparks of light.

"You see," Smith said, "but you don't understand. We said we came from the Outer Darkness, remember? That's it. And those little lights, Norvis, are thousands upon thousands of Great Lights, so far away that it's impossible for me to tell you how far—your language doesn't cover it!"

Norvis dizzily tried to grasp the immensity of the great black abyss he was staring into. Then, out of the corner of the window, there came a line of light, a great curve of glowing radiance. Below it was utter blackness.

"We're taking you out where you can see Nidor; that's your Great Light, shining through the clouds on the other side of your world. We're on the night side now, but we're heading for the day side. We'll have to put filters on the viewport; the Great Light is so bright it would blind you in a few seconds if you looked directly at it."

They showed him the Great Light, and they showed him the huge white ball that was the cloud-covered Nidor. When it was all over, he was sitting again on the little seat, facing the three Earthmen. "It's terrible," he said softly. "We have thought that the Great Light was something that helped us and protected us, but—"

"Just a minute," Davis said. "Don't get the idea we're trying to tell you that there *isn't* Someone who keeps an eye on us all. We, too, have a concept of a Great Being—but if He exists, that ball of gas out there is just part of His handiwork; if He exists He's a lot bigger and grander and more powerful than that star. And, if He exists, your prayers have reached Him, no matter what you call Him."

Norvis nodded, but he knew his faith in the priesthood of the Great Light, small though it had been before, was now completely shattered. "What was your reason for doing all this, Smith?"

The Earthman knotted his fingers together. "Let's look at it this way. A man needs friends. He can't live alone. He must have someone to like and love, and someone or something he can pit himself against. Call it conflict, call it challenge, if you like. Not the bloody conflict of battle, but the friendly conflict of a game. Do you follow?"

Norvis nodded hesitantly.

"Well, we Earthmen need friends too. It's the same thing with a race. Long ago, we were divided into different groups—not true races, for they could interbreed, but differing in skin color and other minor ways. These groups conflicted with one another—sometimes violently—and this conflict helped to make us wiser and stronger because, in watching others we learn more about ourselves.

"We fought and quarreled and argued. We were divided by religious and political beliefs and by skin color, and the battles surged over Earth for many thousands of years. And all the time, we were learning.

We developed weapons so powerful we dared not use them; we conquered space and the battles still went on. But eventually, the inevitable happened.

"The lines of demarcation between the groups began to blur. Political division became meaningless, religious differences were smoothed out, and the various races blended into one. We became a unit. A single, solidified group—the Earthmen. We had conquered our planet and the stars. And ourselves.

"But we lacked something," Smith continued. "We lacked friends. And we lacked conflict. Within a few thousand years, we would stagnate and become static and—eventually—die out. And then we found Nidor. We had searched for another intelligent race for centuries before we found you. Once, we found an intelligent race—vicious, monstrous things whose thinking was so different from ours that we had no common meeting ground. We were forced to destroy them.

"But Nidor was perfect—an intelligent species, not too unlike us, with a way of thinking only slightly different. And there was no question of our ever losing our separate identities as races; Earthmen and Nidorians are too unlike for that. But we had found what we needed. We needed you—and you needed us. You had formed a perfectly static society; it was incredible to us that a society could remain unchanging for so long. So we had to get you to move, to start a dynamic instead of a static civilization."

Smith moistened dry lips. *"We have done that now,"* he said.

"I still don't understand," Norvis said weakly. "You've wrecked us—ruined us. Things will never be the same again. Why didn't you just come down and teach us about your race and your world, instead of all this mummery?"

"It wouldn't have worked. Unless your people developed on their own, they would have been so overwhelmed by us that we could never be equals. So we had to smash your culture—force you to learn to build anew."

"But—to smash us so completely!"

Smith smiled. "We were very gentle, believe me. We could have hit you so hard you'd never have recovered—at least not in time to be of any use to us. What would happen, Norvis, if we'd dumped a few hundred billion weights of cobalt all over Nidor? Or printed up perfect imitations of paper scrip? Or blighted the peych-beans for a century? What would have happened? And there are even worse ways. No. We had to be very careful and handle you gently."

"I—it's incredible, Smith."

The Earthman smiled. "The first thing we needed was a better, cleverer kind of Nidorian—one who could think for himself. So we started the Bel-rogas School. We taught you, and well—but the main purpose was something else.

"Our admission requirements were high. Only very intelligent and very healthy students were admitted. And the School was surrounded by spacious parks filled with romantically secluded nooks. Do you follow me?"

Norvis' face broke into an awed smile. "Great Light! My mother and father met there—and my grandparents! You brought the best of Nidor there to— to *breed* them!"

Smith smiled. "That's a rather crude term for it, but it is selective breeding. Nobody's free will was interfered with—no one was forced into anything. It was simply made very convenient. And we got the result we wanted, Norvis. *You!*"

"*Me?* I am—"

"You're the result of four generations of carefully-controlled genetic manipulation. There are others, of course, but your line was the best. And believe me, you far exceeded our expectations. Tell me—why aren't *you* the Executive Officer of Nidor, instead of Kris peKym?"

"I didn't want it," Norvis said. "I found out years ago that heroes don't live very long. I tried it and damned near got stoned to death for my pains. Since then, I've left the heroics up to hero-types—like Del and Kris."

"And Ganz peDel," Smith added.

Norvis nodded. "I'll probably need Ganz too before long; if Kris peKym keeps up the way he has been, someone's going to slit his throat one of these days. But what's this got to do with your program?"

"Simply that it succeeded better than we expected. Actually, we'd pictured you as the hero. We figured you'd get killed, of course, but not before you'd done your work. As it is, you'll live to a ripe old age, pulling the strings behind the scenes. And it won't be necessary for us to train *your* successor."

"I feel as though *you're* pulling *my* strings," Norvis said.

"In a way, perhaps—but no more than we were manipulating the rest of Nidor. You happened to be an important man, that's all.

"In your grandfather Kiv's time, *he* was important. He was studying the hugl, so we bred a new kind of hugl and started the Great Plague—which he stopped, and, in doing so, made the first big crack in your static culture. Your mother was a Brajjyd, and she married a Brajjyd—another crack in a culture that had forbidden in-clan marriage.

"And you? You found the growth hormone—all by yourself. We knew what would happen, so we pulled you out of a nasty jam and at the same time gave you a good motive for hating us."

"And driving you off the planet," Norvis said.

"Which you did admirably. We haven't done a thing since you appeared—except toss our best students out on their ears and make them hate the school, just as we did you. You've got a lot of smart lads there, Norvis. Make use of them."

Norvis nodded, grinning. "I think I'll build another school—with lots of nice, romantic parks."

Smith laughed. "Good! But remember—we haven't controlled you for years—not since we tossed you out. We gave you a free hand, and, as of now, it will be even freer. We actually have never really controlled you. Even when you were in School, I let you go ahead on your own. Your discovery of the hormone was, as I said, completely your own.

"No—of all people on Nidor, you alone have been completely free to do and think and act as you liked—to do the things that you thought were right for Nidor. We watched, yes—but we have neither helped nor hindered. We simply kept silent and made our preparations to leave Nidor.

"Nidor today is your product, and its future is up to you. For we are leaving—completely."

Norvis chuckled softly. "Funny. I've dedicated fifteen years of my life to driving you Earthmen away, and now that I've done it, I don't want you to go." He looked up into the Earthman's eyes. "I see what you mean. A race needs friends. I *like* you, Smith. And my children's children will like yours."

"I hope so," Smith said. "Now, we must go—and you and I will never see each other again. It's all yours, the whole mess. You've got a broken culture to put together again. You've got at least two heretical religions springing up—the New Lawyer in Lebron, and the group in Sugon. You'll have political factions; you'll have a complete breakup of the Clan system soon. You'll have more riots, more battles, more bloodshed. But keep moving forward. In the end, you'll have something better than the dead Way of your Ancestors."

"Aren't you ever coming back?"

"Not in your lifetime—or mine. Oh, we'll peek in once in a while to check your progress, but we won't touch. This new civilization has to be a Nidorian one—not just a copy of our own. Eventually, you'll build ships like this, and we can meet on even terms—as friends."

"But Nidorians will hate Earthmen for a long time."

"Don't worry about that. We don't really call ourselves by the Nidorian word '*Earthmen*'—our own term means the same, but it sounds completely different. And these beards were grown for a purpose. Nidorians will remember the beards long after they've forgotten everything else. And we don't normally wear beards. No, your people won't know us when they first meet us, and when we finally tell them we'll both have a big laugh on the joke we pulled on their ancestors. We—"

Harrison stood up and glanced at a little machine on his wrist. "Five minutes to rendezvous with the mother ship, Smith. You about through?"

"I think so. Any more questions, Norvis?"

"I don't think so," he said firmly. "I think I understand. I'm ready to go back."

"Good. The rest *is* up to you. I'm going to send you back down alone—think you can take it?"

Norvis nodded. "I've seen so much now that a little drop of a few miles won't hurt me."

"Fine," Smith said. A humorous twinkle came into his eyes. "By the way, don't think you're going to get away with the force-field generator. When you get down, take it off and throw it away. We're going to destroy it, and you don't want to be anywhere near it when we do."

Norvis grinned. "I won't be."

24

He wasn't. When his feet touched the ground only a few feet from where he had tethered his deest, he felt the force-field die. Quickly, he unstrapped the generator from his waist and hurled it away into the rocks.

Then he mounted the animal and rode westward, not even looking backward when a silent burst of light illuminated the landscape around him. The Earthmen were gone.

He rode slowly, his mind still dazed. He had gone to the Mountains of the Morning to find out the secret of the Earthmen—and he had found. The magnitude of the Earthmen's plan dazzled him. He rode on, revolving the concept in his mind.

Nidor was a mess, as Smith had said. But it could soon be straightened out; it—

And then, quite suddenly, as though the Great Light Himself had given full illumination to his mind, Norvis peRahn Brajjyd realized the enormity of the terrible thing he had done.

He had done.

He.

The Earthmen hadn't ruined Nidor—no, not at all. Everything they had done had healed itself. The hugl plague had done nothing really drastic to Nidor; in a hundred or two hundred years, it would have been forgotten. The discovery of the growth hormone had done nothing in the long run; it, too, would have vanished away in the mists of the monotonous history of Nidor.

Who had started the Merchants' Party, and thus conceived for the people of Nidor the idea that there could be more than one group contending for supremacy? Who?

Norvis peRahn Brajjyd.

Who had begun, secretly, the little splinter groups of religion that now threatened the whole Nidorian culture?

Who?

Norvis peRahn Brajjyd.

Who had engineered the rebellion against the Earthmen? Who had actually caused the burning of the School? Who had started the agitation of the crazed masses who had burned and destroyed the Great Temple? Who had instituted the idea that Nidorians should be led by a single popular strong man instead of a senile Council of Elders?

Who had ruined, beyond any hope of redemption, the culture, the mores, the ideals of Nidor?

Who?

Norvis peRahn Brajjyd!

There was bitterness in his mouth and in his mind as he realized the full truth of what the Earthman had told him.

The process was irreversible; Nidor could never go back to the Way of the Ancestors. That Way implied a certain innocence—an ignorance of other ways. But

Norvis had introduced too many new ideas. A culture which had once been static had become dynamic because it had been overburdened with new ideas and concepts.

It wasn't catastrophes that had ruined Nidor—not even the Great Cataclysm had done that. It had been *ideas*—devastatingly new ideas—that had done the terrible, irreparable damage to a culture which had sustained itself intact for thousands and thousands of years.

For a decade and a half, Norvis had hated the Earthmen for what they had done. Then, when Smith had explained, he had thought that they were doing it—*had* done it—for the good of Nidor, and he had felt relief.

But now he knew that the Earthmen had done nothing directly. They had simply bred—yes, *bred!*—a Nidorian who would do their work for them. And he had. As they had known he would.

He didn't know, at that point, whether he hated Smith or worshipped him—or, perhaps, feared him.

He decided it must be hatred, but it wouldn't do him any good to hate Earthmen. He was helpless, as they had known he would be. He had to rebuild Nidor—rebuild it along the lines they wanted. Why? Because he was built that way; he could do nothing else. He couldn't stand around and watch his home, his people, dissolve into barbarism.

He was irrevocably dedicated to the course ahead of him.

Damn them, he thought. *Damn them!* And then, after a moment: *Bless their damned souls!*

It was the night of the second day when he arrived in Holy Gelusar. The Great City looked oddly unimportant now, no longer the metropolis he had once thought it to be. He trotted across the Bridge of Gon and headed toward the Great Temple.

No sooner did he approach the charred building when a guard rushed up. "Secretary Norvis! Where have you been? We've looked all over Nidor for you!"

"What's happened?" Norvis asked. It was near morning, and he was tired.

"Leader Kris has been shot!"

"Take me to him!" Norvis said. He dismounted and the guard led him up the stairs to the room where Kris lay. His fingers quivered a little as he threw open the door.

Marja was standing at the foot of the bed, and Ganz by the Leader's side. Two other men that Norvis recognized as physicians stood by helplessly.

Norvis glanced at one of them. "How's his condition?"

"Serious," the physician said bleakly. He lowered his voice. "We don't have much hope."

Kris, Norvis thought sadly. *You were almost a son to me—and here you are, dying of the bullet I should have gotten.*

He took Kris' cool limp hand. The Leader opened his eyes slowly and focussed them on Norvis.

"I heard what that doctor said," he muttered indistinctly. "Not much hope. You don't have to hide it from me."

"Easy, Kris," Norvis said. "Don't talk."

"Doesn't matter. I'm going. Maybe it's best this way—cut off at the top. Wealthy, good wife, everyone cheering. Earthmen gone. Nidor rebuilding. I might have lived to see worse." His head sank back. "You've been good to me, Norvis. Thanks."

Kris shuddered, and Norvis squeezed his hand and let it drop. "He's dead," Norvis said. There was little emotion apparent in his voice.

"He was a great man," Ganz peDel said. Behind him, Marja sobbed quietly.

Norvis took a deep breath and steeled himself for what had to be done. He rose from the bedside, walked toward Ganz peDel, put his arm around the boy's broad shoulders.

"Nidor needs a new Leader," he said quietly.

"But I'm—you—I—"

Norvis smiled. "Kris thought you could do the job, Ganz peDel. Do *you?*"

"I—I think so," Ganz said, after a pause.

"Good. We've got plenty of work ahead of us, then." Norvis walked to the window of the death-room and threw open the shutters. The Great Light had just risen, and the light of dawn came streaming in, breaking through the eternal clouds of Nidor.